"WORDS FAIL ME." DEIL'S VOICE WAS HUSKY. "YOU LOOK . . ."

"All right?"

"Definitely all right," he confirmed, in that same husky tone.

"Good?"

"Better than good."

"Gorgeous, ravishing, 'fantabulous'!?" she teasingly suggested.

"You're all of the above."

"So are you."

"Why thank you, roomie!"

Kelly came closer and realized that the added inches of her heels had made them the same height.

Deil, noting the same thing, murmured, "For once we see eye to eye."

"Enjoy it while you can," she impudently suggested.

"Oh, I intend to."

A CANDLELIGHT ECSTASY ROMANCE ®

A
SUMMER'S
EMBRACE

Cathie Linz

A CANDLELIGHT ECSTASY ROMANCE ®

*For my mom, who taught
me never to forget the simple
pleasures of a new box of crayons!
With special thanks to De Fu.*

To Our Readers:

We have been delighted with your enthusiastic response to Candlelight Ecstasy Romances®, and we thank you for the interest you have shown in this exciting series.

In the upcoming months we will continue to present the distinctive sensuous love stories you have come to expect only from Ecstasy. We look forward to bringing you many more books from your favorite authors and also, the very finest work from new authors of contemporary romantic fiction.

As always we are striving to present the unique, absorbing love stories that you enjoy most—books that are more than ordinary romance.

Your suggestions and comments are always welcome. Please write to us at the address below.

Sincerely,

The Editors
Candlelight Romances
1 Dag Hammarskjold Plaza
New York, New York 10017

CHAPTER ONE

"There's no way you can stay here!" Kelly Watson firmly informed her roommate's business-suited brother.

"Of course there is," the man who'd introduced himself as Deil Foster replied. "The apartment has two bedrooms."

"That's irrelevant. You can't stay here."

Deil looked unconcerned with her refusal. "Why not? Have you already sublet Sally's room?"

"I wouldn't do that," Kelly angrily protested. "Sally's already paid her share of the rent through August."

"Which means the room belongs to her?"

"That's right." Finally he was seeing the light.

"Then there's no problem. Sally invited me to come stay here while she's in my flat in London."

Kelly wearily sank onto a wicker-backed rocking chair and stared at her unexpected visitor. How could Sally have done this to her? "Why wasn't I consulted?"

"At a guess, I'd say that she wanted to avoid an argument."

"Why should she invite you to stay here when you've got a perfectly good apartment in London?" Kelly questioned in a suspicious tone.

9

Deil's hazel eyes narrowed dangerously. "Are you accusing me of lying?"

"I'm not accusing you of anything except coming into my apartment uninvited."

"But I was invited." He relaxed again. "By Sally. She gave me the key."

"Without my permission or approval," Kelly instantly pointed out.

"Look, I didn't want to bring this up but . . . my sister did you a favor when you were homeless."

Damn Sally's loose tongue! How much of her private life had been recounted for Deil Foster's amusement? Kelly sat up a little straighter, her manner distant. "She was looking for a roommate."

"At a time when you desperately needed one."

Kelly closed her green eyes, mentally blocking out the man across from her and reviewing Sally's departure from Denver's international airport three days ago. No mention had been made of her brother coming to Colorado.

But here he was, his speech clipped and precise, his suit rumpled. He looked and sounded utterly foreign in the Rocky Mountain playground of Aspen. Yet Kelly knew he was an American, a journalist who'd been based in London for the past several years. Sally had told her that much, but she hadn't bothered letting her in on this little plan.

Well, Deil Foster would just have to stay somewhere else. It didn't matter if he was Sally's brother. Kelly had never met him before and had no intention of sharing her apartment with him.

Her eyes snapped open, ready to do battle. "Look, there are a lot of rentals here in Aspen. I'm sure you can find a condominium available for the summer."

"Why should I find a condominium when I already have this apartment?"

"You don't have this apartment!" Kelly didn't know how she could make it any clearer than that.

"Where's the bathroom?" Deil suddenly straightened to ask.

"The second door down the hall," she automatically replied. "But . . ."

He was gone before she could complete her sentence. Damn! Kelly had been in a rush that morning and the bathroom was still in a mess. Too bad. Maybe it would make Deil think twice about having her as a roommate.

Her rocking became more agitated as she mulled over her predicament. Apartment rentals were hard to come by in exclusive Aspen. A large portion of the real estate was set aside for daily or weekly tourist rentals, with no long-term options. Deil was right; Sally had been there when Kelly had desperately needed a place. But it had been a fair exchange—Sally hadn't been able to swing the rent alone either.

The apartment was perfect, not one of those sterile boxlike buildings, but a renovated Victorian mansion. Kelly had fallen in love with the neatly painted red house on first sight. Their unit, one of four, was on the top floor and reached by a white-trimmed outer staircase. A matching white picket fence surrounded the pocket-size front lawn.

This was her home, hers and Sally's. Not hers and Deil's. The sound of the bathroom door opening halted her rocking. Her shoulders braced, her conviction firm, she rose to face Deil. His hand was braced on the hallway's doorjamb, his face gray.

Her arguments fled as she took in his unhealthy appearance. "Are you all right?" she asked in concern.

"I'm fine."

He was obviously lying through his teeth, but Kelly saw no advantage to pointing out that fact. Besides, she already had a good idea what might be wrong with him. "How did you get here?" was her first question.

Deil unsteadily made his way back to the couch, sitting down with care. "I drove."

"All the way from Denver?"

"No, from the airport."

"Pitkin airport?"

He leaned back, gingerly resting his head on the sofa cushions. "I don't know what the name of the damn airport is."

"You mean you just changed planes in Denver and flew directly here to Aspen?"

He nodded wearily, closing his eyes after doing so.

"That explains it then."

His eyes crept open. "Explains what?"

"You've got all the symptoms of altitude sickness." Kelly listed them on her slender fingers. "Nausea, dizziness, stomach upset, headache."

"All I need is some rest," he muttered, getting back to his feet.

"Where are you going?" After asking she realized it might not have been a tactful question in light of his physically distressed state.

But Deil wasn't headed for the bathroom. He picked up a travel-worn leather suitcase and strode down the hall toward Sally's bedroom.

"Where are you going?" she repeated, following him.

"I'm going to bed."

"You can't go to bed!" she sputtered from her position on the threshold.

"Watch me," he invited, discarding his jacket and loosening his tie.

Kelly stubbornly stood her ground, even after he'd peeled off his shirt. If he expected her to bolt at the sight of his nude body, he was in for a surprise. Kelly had four brothers, two younger, two older, and had seen them all in various stages of undress. In addition to that, she'd taken life drawing classes all through college and sketched many a nude male model.

Observing her belligerent stance, Deil hesitated in carrying out his intended threat. His hands hovered over the zipper on his trousers and then stilled. Anger hardened his expression as he curtly stated, "The show's over."

"Oh, and just when it was getting interesting too," she cooed.

His answer was to firmly shut the door in her face.

Kelly wasn't very proud of her behavior. After all, Deil was Sally's only brother. What with the long transatlantic flight and then the bumpy air commuter ride, he'd suffered enough for one day. She could afford to be generous and let him stay the night. That decision made, she knocked on the closed door.

Deil wrenched it open, his expression bordering on glowering. "What?"

"Would you like some camomile tea? It'll help settle your stomach."

He eyed her suspiciously. "What are you planning on doing, putting arsenic in it?"

"Not unless you prefer it that way," she gibed with a grin.

"Then thanks." He broke into a smile for the first time

13

since she'd met him. It changed his entire face, displaying a set of laugh lines that led her to believe he must usually smile quite a lot. "I would like some tea. And hold the arsenic, please."

Fifteen minutes later Kelly brought a carefully prepared tray into Sally's bedroom. Rose-tinted twilight crept in through the open windows and softened the features of the man sleeping in the single bed. She set the tray on the dresser and carefully pulled the windows shut. Even during the summer the nights got chilly. It was only early June, and snow still covered the mountain peaks.

She stood beside the bed, openly studying his slumbering figure. Dark wavy hair fell across a wide forehead in what Kelly was tempted to describe as bangs, but the term seemed inappropriate when used in reference to a man. And Deil Foster was most definitely a man, a very attractive one! His physique was firm and muscular without being burly and somewhat on the slim side. Must be all that airplane food, Kelly thought to herself with an irrepressible grin.

Muttering something unintelligible, Deil turned in his sleep, startling Kelly. She retreated, closing the drapes and gathering up the tray before leaving the cozy confines of the darkened room. The evening hours were spent refining her latest designs and absently munching her way through a large piece of turkey-and-broccoli quiche. She went to bed a little after eleven.

Crash! Kelly jerked awake, groggy eyes automatically fastening on the time. 3:02 A.M. Had she been dreaming, or had someone broken into the apartment? No, the muffled curses she now heard had a decidedly British inflection to them. Pulling on the cotton Japanese kimono she used as a robe, she went in search of her uninvited guest. Light switches were clicked on along the way. She found him in the living room, donned in a blue terry-cloth robe. Her artist's eye lingered to appreciate his muscular legs.

"What are you doing?" Kelly's demand came out as a whisper, for something about the dead of night made it seem appropriate to speak in hushed tones.

Deil, however, felt no such compunction. "I was looking for the kitchen," he growled, righting the piece of furniture he'd knocked over.

"It's not under the table." She was unable to resist teasing Deil.

He slashed her a look that was somewhere between irritation and exasperation. "Are you usually this clever in the middle of the night?"

"Without fail." Her voice dripped with sarcasm. "I adore being woken out of a sound sleep by a horrendous crash!"

"Personally, I can think of more enjoyable ways to wake up," he murmured, his eyes gleaming in the half-light.

Kelly gazed at him in surprise. She'd had him pegged as a hard-bitten reporter—cynical, sarcastic, and cold. That image didn't allow for seductive humor.

"I'd rather sleep," she retorted in what she hoped was a deflating put-down.

"Then go on back to bed." He waved her away. "I'll just make myself a little something to eat."

Kelly ruefully shook her head. "After what you've done to the living room, I'm not sure it's safe to let you into the kitchen!"

His brow furrowed with impatience, his glare directed

15

at the piece of furniture he'd stumbled into. "Whose idea was it to stick this flimsy table in a high traffic area?"

"Your sister's."

"Figures," was his wry response. "It seems like she's always trying to trip me up."

"She seems to be quite successful at it too."

"Please," Deil groaned, putting a hand to his head. "No more verbal battles. I'm light-headed from hunger."

"And from the altitude," Kelly tacked on. "Aspen's nearly eight thousand feet up, you know. You should take it easy for the first day or so. Come on, I'll make you a sandwich."

Deil followed her into what turned out to be an extremely compact kitchen. He looked around in dismayed amusement. "What was this before the house was renovated? A closet?"

"Probably," she absently agreed, gathering bread and butter. "Not a vegetarian, are you?"

He shook his head, hungrily eyeing the plate of sliced ham she slid out of the miniature refrigerator. "Sally's the only vegetarian in the family; the rest of us are all normal."

"Don't insult your sister," she reprimanded, brandishing the bread knife with a threatening flourish.

Deil laughingly retreated a step or two, which was as far as he could go without banging into the stove. "Sally told me you were a loyal friend."

"I like to think so," Kelly nodded.

"She also told me that you're an artist. What do you do? Drawings? Paintings?"

"Stained glass."

"Stained glass?" he echoed.

"You seem surprised."

16

"I've never met a stained glass artist before." He made her sound like a creature from another age.

"Then we're even." She flipped down the space-saver table that was hinged on the wall. "I've never met a journalist before."

Deil pulled up a chair. "I thought stained glass was a lost art," he mused, taking a bite of the sandwich she placed before him.

"That's a rumor that we started to keep the competition down!"

"Clever marketing technique," he stated before adding, "Pull up a chair and join me."

She pulled up a stool instead, and sat across from him. In such close quarters it was inevitable that her knee should bump against his. The accidental contact initiated an amazingly strong chain reaction, until a myriad of energized molecules were flying beneath her skin. Responding reflexively, Kelly jerked her legs away, gliding her bare foot over his in the process. By now the energized current had traveled the length of her leg and beyond, setting up a warm wave of sexual awareness.

Disconcerted, Kelly checked Deil's face for any signs of a matching reaction, but he seemed totally engrossed in finishing his midnight snack.

"That was a great sandwich," he enthused. "Even the bread was good!"

"It's homemade."

"You made it?"

"Me?" She laughingly shook her head at the very idea. Cooking was not her forte. "No. I work in a café and occasionally they let me bring home the day-old bakery items."

"Wherever it came from, I enjoyed it. Thank you."

17

"Would you like your camomile tea now?"

"You know what I'd really like?" Without warning, his voice lowered, throbbing with hungry intensity.

Kelly was almost afraid to ask. "What?"

"A glass of fresh-squeezed orange juice."

"Orange juice?" How anticlimactic!

"Mmm. European orange juice just doesn't taste the same."

"It didn't take you long to make an inventory of the contents of my icebox," she remarked.

His expression was one of assumed modesty. "That's my journalistic eye at work, automatically noting every detail."

"What paper do you work for?" Kelly inquired while pouring him the requested juice.

"I freelance."

"Oh."

Deil took the proffered glass. "Why the disappointed 'oh'? You don't think a freelance journalist is real?"

"You look real enough to me," she returned, watching him down the juice in three huge swallows.

"I'll take that as a compliment," he smiled.

"And I'll take your empty glass. Did you want more orange juice?"

"Yes, please."

"You must've been in London quite some time to pick up such an accent."

"What accent?"

"Your English accent."

"I don't have an English accent," he denied in amazement.

"You sure do. So much so, that you could pose as my English butler!"

18

"Make me an offer!" A devilish gleam lightened his hazel eyes.

"If I ever get rich enough to afford a butler, you'll be on the top of the list."

"I suppose I can't ask for more than that. At least not on such short acquaintance."

Kelly pretended not to hear that last remark, efficiently dumping the dirty dishes in the stainless steel sink. "Shall we go back to bed now?"

"Certainly. Yours or mine?"

How like a man! Had he known her better, the curve of Kelly's smile would have warned Deil that he was in big trouble. As it was, she had the benefit of surprise on her side.

"I make it a practice not to seduce men suffering from jet lag and altitude sickness. If it had been just one or the other you might have had a chance, but as it is . . ." She eyed him with ridiculing regret before pivoting on her heel and leaving.

Unfortunately, Kelly's grand exit was sabotaged by her kimono, which was too long for her five-foot-seven frame. The hem needed to be taken up, but she kept putting the job off. The trailing material extracted its revenge by tripping her up.

She fell backward against a living wall of muscular strength. The warmth of bare skin permeated right through her thin cotton wrap. Was that her heart skittering like a wild thing, or his? Not that it mattered; Kelly didn't intend staying in his arms long enough to find out. But shaky legs refused to do her mind's bidding.

"Trying to knock me off my feet, Miss Watson?" The teasing question was aimed at her ear, his breath stirring the downy softness of her hair while his warmly amusing tone plied her senses.

"Perhaps I was trying to knock some sense into you," she sweetly countered.

"An unusual approach."

"It wasn't an approach. I tripped."

"I noticed."

"I'm all right now. You can let me go." The cool request was accompanied by a pointed glance at the hands still gripping her shoulders.

"Certainly." Deil released her and watched in amusement as she marched out of the room, this time not missing a step.

It was almost five before Kelly fell asleep again, and then she had to get up at eight. The apartment was quiet, her uninvited roommate sleeping soundly, no doubt. Kelly turned the shower on stronger than usual, knowing the pipes rattled like a geyser. If the noise disturbed the still-snoozing Deil, he lodged no audible protests. Dressed in beige chinos and a light blue shirt, she hurried into the kitchen to whip up her nutritious breakfast drink.

Kelly didn't hear Deil's arrival over the blender's whirring. His suit had been exchanged for a well-fitting pair of jeans and a navy polo shirt. The casual attire showed him in a different light. Gone was the exhausted man in the travel-wrinkled suit, and in his place was more of the teasing devil she'd encountered at three in the morning.

"Where are you off to so early?"

She poured out her drink before answering. "Work."

"The café?"

"No, the gallery."

"I thought you said you worked in a café."

"I do. I also work in a gallery. A friend of mine lets me

20

share her studio in exchange for my minding the front store for her a couple days a week. This is one of those days."

"How do you keep your schedule straight?"

Kelly pointed to a large calendar hanging on the wall. "I write it all down."

"What's zip dip?" she heard him ask.

"Zip dip?"

"That's what it says," he maintained, pointing to her writing.

She stopped on her way back from the sink to translate. "International design festival."

Deil read on. "Who's Barry?"

Kelly ignored the question, checking the display on the digital watch hanging on a golden chain around her neck. "Damn, I'm late! Sorry I won't have time to help you find other accommodations, but I'd suggest starting with the visitors' center. Feel free to use my phone, so long as the calls are local. The phonebook's over there on the top shelf."

"Thank you, but I won't need it."

"You've thought of someplace else to stay?"

"I've no intention of leaving."

"What do you mean?"

"Exactly what I said."

"I don't have time to go over this with you again. I thought you got the message last night. You were sick, so out of the kindness of my heart I let you stay. Now it's time for you to leave."

"Aren't you late?" he reminded her.

She was, and Bonnie was counting on her to open the gallery this morning. Frustrated beyond belief, Kelly warned, "I'll be back at two. I hope you'll be gone by then!"

He mockingly inclined his head. "Hope, by all means, but I'll still be here." He waited until she was halfway out the door before adding, "Have a nice day, roomie!"

CHAPTER TWO

The day was sunny, the scenery gorgeous, but Kelly was immune to both. How dare Deil Foster insist on staying in her apartment. So much for being a good Samaritan. She should have kicked him out last night!

There wasn't time to take her bike out of storage, so she marched the three blocks to Bonnie's gallery, cutting across the picturesque pedestrian mall. A computer-controlled fountain performed its daily dips and splashes against the stunning backdrop of Aspen Mountain. Usually the picture-perfect setting brought a smile to Kelly's lips whenever she passed it. But not today. Today she wished Aspen weren't so special and apartments weren't so expensive!

It was four minutes after nine when Kelly unlocked the front door of Artisans. Its location, right across the street from the popular mall, insured a brisk business. As she did each time she opened the gallery, Kelly marveled at her streak of good luck in finding studio space available to share.

Bonnie Cherinsky was a very talented potter. Her work was practical, yet touched with a sense of whimsy which made it very popular. Bonnie had delivered twins three months ago, and had her hands full with them, so the time she could spend minding the store was understandably limited. Her suggestion that Kelly share the studio in exchange for working in the gallery had been eagerly accepted. Besides the space, Bonnie also had a kiln, a luxury Kelly had always hoped for.

Since then Kelly had been able to double her commissions and still have time to make a number of small pieces to sell in the gallery. Renovators were beginning to seek out her help in restoring some of the stained glass windows in Aspen's numerous Victorian buildings. If things continued on their present course, by next year she could be in a financial position to devote all her time to her craft.

The morning was busy with interested customers strolling in and out, some buying, some merely looking. Kelly had just completed a sale when she saw Barry enter the gallery.

"Hi." She greeted him with friendly pleasure.

It was not returned. "How long have you been living with that guy?" Barry's conventionally handsome face was flushed with anger as he shouted the question.

"Would you lower your voice?" she hissed, feeling the curious stares of several browsing customers.

"Not until you answer me. Who the hell is that guy?"

"Deil Foster."

"Foster?" Barry repeated in a quieter tone.

"That's right. Sally's brother."

"I thought she went to visit him in London."

"So did I."

"Then what's he doing here, living with you?"

"He's not living with me!" Kelly protested angrily, drawing more attention to herself.

"Then what would you call it?"

"He's using Sally's room."

24

"For what?"

Kelly slashed him a reproving stare. "To sleep in, of course."

"Alone?"

"I only met him yesterday." Her reply was icy. "Does that answer your question?"

Barry had the grace to look a little shamefaced. "It threw me when this guy informed me that he's your new roommate. If you're going to live with any man, it had better be me." Barry had already invited her to move in with him several times during the two months since she'd met him. As an independently successful investment advisor, he was very much a part of Aspen's "good life." He worked out of a spacious home he had custom-built for him in the hills behind town. His schedule was flexible, planned around his rigorous athletic activities.

It took Kelly almost half an hour to soothe Barry's anger, which Deil had no doubt deliberately aroused. Her own anger was fueled by this calculated troublemaking. She got home at two in the afternoon and found Deil in the kitchen.

"What are you doing here?"

"I'm making lunch," Deil calmly replied.

"With *my* food?"

"Technically, I suppose it's your food. In the future, though, I thought we'd split the food bill down the middle. Then it would be *our* food. Seems more reasonable than buying two lots of everything."

"We don't have a future!"

Deil paused in his culinary preparations to slant her an indulgent smile. "My, we're in a bad mood this afternoon, aren't we?"

"Yes," she agreed, ignoring the friendly warmth of his

hazel eyes. "And it's going to get worse if you don't leave."

His expression became serious. "Kelly, I told you I'm not leaving. I can't."

"Can't? Or won't?" she challenged.

"Come sit down and we'll talk about it."

Kelly settled into her wicker rocking chair, leaving the sofa for Deil. She'd listen to what he said and then toss him out. He didn't have a legal leg to stand on.

"I suppose I should've gone into more detail about my circumstances last night," he began.

Her mind was immediately speculating as to what those circumstances might be. "You're broke," was her first guess, having been hit for loans before.

"No, I'm not broke," Deil huffily denied. "I'm finishing a rather controversial book on English politics and word got out about it. A number of people in high places want to know what I'm going to say about them. I wasn't able to get any of the necessary revisions done due to the constant interruptions. So I came here. Far enough from England that no one will bother me."

"I don't see why you can't spend the summer in some other apartment."

"I said I wasn't broke; that doesn't mean I'm wealthy. Frankly, I can't afford the exorbitant rents charged for short-term rentals."

"That's *your* problem." Kelly strived to sound callously indifferent.

Apparently she succeeded, for Deil suddenly got angry, but it was an anger iced with sarcasm. "What are you afraid of? That I'm going to attack you? Because if that's it, you can relax. I made the mistake of getting involved

26

with one of my sister's roommates once before. It's not an experience I'd ever want to repeat."

"You may say that now, but . . ."

"I can assure you that I'm not all that pleased about the prospect of sharing this apartment with you. Sally implied that you'd be gone most of the time and that I'd practically have the place to myself. Those were the conditions I agreed to when I let her have my flat in London in exchange for supposed solitude in Aspen. Female roommates are nothing but trouble. They start getting possessive and before you know it they're hearing wedding bells."

"You speak as if from experience. Are you married?" It hadn't occurred to Kelly to ask before.

"No, I'm not married, and I don't intend to be until I'm in my mid-thirties. By then I should be established as a writer and be ready to start a family. But for now I treasure my freedom. The last time I got involved with one of Sally's roommates, the girl had her china pattern picked out before I made her understand that. Not only did she nearly scratch my eyes out, but Sally didn't speak to me for six months. It was horribly awkward for all involved. Speaking of awkwardness, I suggest that we negotiate a set of house rules so that our term as roommates can be completed with as little difficulty as possible." Deil got up to hand her a blank sheet of paper and pencil. "Let's make a list. I'll list all the things I don't want you to do, and you list all the things you don't want me to do. Then we'll discuss any disagreements and hammer out a compromise."

"I'm not sure this page will be large enough," she sniped, a bit overwhelmed by the way Deil was taking charge of the situation.

Deil smiled as if he found her anger amusing. "Then use the back."

Realizing that any further comment would be superfluous, Kelly drew her feet up onto her chair seat and balanced the paper on her bent knees. She knew from experience that she concentrated best in this semi-scrunched position. They both finished their lists at about the same time, which surprised her because she couldn't imagine how Deil could come up with that many things about her. But he did.

Kelly was still gazing in disbelief at the page-long list he'd drawn up, when he began. "My first complaint is that you didn't spell my name correctly. It may be pronounced Deel but it's spelled D-e-i-l."

"Where did you get a name like that anyway?" she demanded, embarrassed by her honest mistake.

Deil attempted to look modest. "My mother gave it to me."

"Obviously." Kelly paused to maintain control of her frazzled patience. "Where did she get it from?"

"The dictionary. My parents are walking encyclopedias of information."

"If your name's in the dictionary, it must have a definition."

"Mmm." His grin was laced with mischievous humor. "Scottish for devil."

"I should've guessed," she sighed. "Shall we get back to the ground rules?"

"By all means."

"I don't understand item number six: Don't touch floppy discs. Who's got floppy discs?"

"I do."

"You have back trouble?" She frowned in confusion.

28

Deil made no attempt to restrain his mirth. It was several moments before he could say, "Back trouble . . . that's a good one!"

By then Kelly was really steaming. What the hell was so funny about back trouble?

Noticing her explosive expression, Deil decided he'd better explain, and quickly too. "I don't have a bad back. Floppy discs are flexible diskettes used for recording information by computers."

"You've got a computer?"

"It's a portable word processor, actually," he corrected with British-like accuracy. "You don't sound as though you approve. Do you object to computers in the home?"

"No," she tartly denied. "Not as long as they can be house-trained and taught to speak our language."

"How generous of you," he mocked.

"I am too generous," she acknowledged.

"Funny, I'd never have guessed it from this rigid set of rules you've written down."

"You weren't exactly brief yourself." She waved his pageful of writing. How had he come up with all these little details? Most were things that wouldn't occur to someone living alone. "Have you done this before?"

His eyes widened with boyish innocence. "Done what?"

"Had a female roommate?"

"I don't rent and tell." There was nothing boyish about his suggestive inflection.

"Cute," she complimented in an uncomplimentary tone. "Your list of restrictions doesn't include 'no questions about past.' "

"Add that as item thirty-four," he instructed.

"Sorry, you've exceeded the limit." She paused to re-

29

view the page, returning to the beginning. "I see we agree on item number three: No smoking."

"And item number two: No streaking."

She looked up in surprise. "I didn't say that."

"Streaking is allowed?" Deil's question was voiced with laughable hopefulness.

"No."

"I should hope not." He surprised her by concurring. She suspected the English accent was played up to stress his supposed decorum. "I came to Aspen to get some work done. With a scantily dressed female traipsing about, I wouldn't be able to do much."

I'll bet you'd be able to do plenty! The thought was so clear that for a moment Kelly was afraid that she'd actually spoken the words aloud. But thankfully some self-preservation system must have locked her tongue.

The area of bringing friends to the apartment brought up the worst battle. Kelly decided to begin with a frontal attack. "Why did you try to make trouble with Barry?"

Deil pointed a finger at his chest in a gesture that suggested "who me?"

"Don't bother denying it. You knew how Barry would take the news that you were staying here. He came by the gallery absolutely furious. It took me half an hour to calm him down."

If Kelly expected this bit of news to incite remorse, she was wrong. Deil actually looked very close to smug. "The excitable type, is he?"

"No, quite the opposite, as a matter of fact."

"What does this Barry do? Is he a ski instructor?"

"Someone like you would think everyone in Aspen is a ski instructor. However, Barry is an investment advisor."

"Wealthy?"

"That's none of your business," she bristled.

"I was just checking to see if you might soon be in a position to hire an English butler. You did say that when you were rich enough to afford one, I'd be at the top of the list."

"I said *if* I ever got rich enough, not *when.*"

"Ah, I see. Hasn't proposed yet, has he?"

"What happened to item thirty-four: No questions about past?"

"You told me I couldn't add that one. Besides, Barry is in your present, not your past."

"Since I see quite a lot of Barry, you'll have to judge him for yourself."

"I'll do that," Deil promised.

"I meant judge in the figurative sense."

"I thought we'd decided that as roommates it would be best not to discuss the figurative senses."

"You think you're so clever." Her purring inflection turned the adjective into a derisive taunt. "Is it because you're a journalist?"

"That's not the only reason, no. What kind of name is Barry Loose anyway?"

"It's spelled L-u-c-e."

"I don't care how it's spelled; the meaning is clear."

When it came to names, Deil was hardly in a position to throw stones, and she told him so. "People in glass houses . . ."

"Is that what we're living in, my dear Watson?"

Kelly ignored his teasing play on her name. "Listen, Deil. I don't want you hassling Barry when he comes over here."

"Is he so weak you have to protect him from me?"

Kelly's face lit up with a smile of genuine amusement.

31

"Barry's more than capable of taking care of himself."
Thinking of his carefully honed muscular body, she had
to add, "You might be the one in need of protection."

Deil eyed her warily. There was something about the
mirthful satisfaction of her expression that warned him to
beware. Wisely deciding that he'd taunted her long
enough, he returned to the subject of their agreement. "So
it's decided then? We share utility and food bills down the
middle."

"With the exception of long-distance calls on the phone
bill," she clarified. "Then whoever made the call has to
pay the charges."

"Agreed."

They made sure both copies matched, with the new
revisions and compromises added. When Kelly mockingly
inquired if Deil planned on printing their agreement out
on his word processor, he replied, "I don't have the printer
with me."

"Then how can you get any work done?"

"I transfer the information over the phone lines."

"In that case it's just as well we clarified the billing
procedure for Rocky Mountain Bell. Are you ready to
sign this now?"

"Yes, I'm ready to sign, even though I do think it's
rather punctilious of you to mention details like toothpaste."

"Punctilious?"

"Attentive to details," he defined.

"You should come wrapped with a dictionary," she
muttered, angry that he'd made her feel stupid.

"Why should I come wrapped at all? Am I a present?"

"You're present in my apartment," was her rapid-fire
retort.

"*Our* apartment," he corrected.

"Temporarily."

"For the rest of the summer." Deil signed his name with sure strokes. "Your turn."

Kelly's hand didn't falter as she placed her signature above his.

"Shall we toast our new agreement?" he suggested.

"With what? I don't have any alcohol in the house."

"With toasted cheese sandwiches?" Deil had to duck quickly in order to avoid the pillow that sailed across the room at him. He lifted both hands in mocking surrender, impressed by her accurate aim. "*Pax.* No more puns."

The living room was small, so the furniture had to follow suit. Besides the sofa, rocking chair, and end tables, there was little room for much else. Even the dining table was small, a Danish import that opened to normal size. They ate lunch on its smooth teak surface.

"Tell me all about stained glass," Deil asked before hungrily digging into his tuna fish sandwich.

Kelly attempted to outline her work briefly, but soon became more involved. "The restoration of glass windows is the most challenging thing I've done, but creating my own work is the most exciting. To see your cartoon take shape—"

"Cartoon?" he repeated after a swallow, certain he must have misunderstood her.

"The pattern," she explained. "You see, it all starts with a design, a working drawing. That drawing becomes a cartoon when the lines are blacked in one-sixteenth of an inch thick. Then you're ready to cut."

"Why one-sixteenth of an inch?"

"Because that's the thickness of the calm."

"The calm? As in 'before the storm'?"

"No, as in lead for leading glass."

She went on about the importance of accurate cutting, tapping, and separation. Deil was an attentive listener, and his questions showed a genuine interest. Kelly was in her element; she loved talking about her work.

"Under that fiery exterior you must possess a wealth of patience," he decided when she'd finished talking about soldering and puttying.

"There'll be a test at the end of this lecture," was her teasing warning.

"A cartoon is a drawing or a design," he dutifully repeated.

"Not 'Peanuts' or 'Doonesbury'?"

"Actually my tastes run more toward mysteries."

"I gathered that much."

"You did?"

Kelly's nod was accompanied by a grin. "The my-dear-Watson routine."

"A dead giveaway, eh?"

"I hope not." She shuddered delicately.

Deil groaned in protest. "I thought we'd decided to declare a moratorium on puns."

"I just wanted to even up the score a little."

"Consider it evened," he instructed. "Now, what were we talking about before you decided to get punny?"

"You were telling me about Sherlock Holmes," she replied, not altogether truthfully.

"Haven't you been teased about your name before?"

She shook her head. "Guess I've never run across any mystery freaks."

"I resent being referred to as a freak. I can see I should've made provisions for a grievance procedure in our agreement."

34

"Now you sound like a union leader."

"Blame it on my tenure in London."

"No, I think it's an integral part of your nature to be a rabble rouser."

"First a mystery freak, then a rabble rouser. Where will it all end?"

"With you going back to your flat in England," she promptly responded.

"You're lucky I'm not a sensitive fellow, or your constant attempts to get rid of me might hurt my feelings." His male countenance wore a suitably woebegone expression. "And after I've only just arrived too. You should be ashamed."

"I don't have anything against you personally," she was saying when he interrupted with, "That's encouraging."

"It wasn't meant to be."

"I know. But around here I can see I'm going to have to grab what encouragement I can."

"I wouldn't recommend grabbing."

"You prefer begging?" The question was accompanied by a flick of a dark eyebrow.

"There's a happy in-between," she countered.

"I know that. Does Barry?"

"You don't really expect me to answer that, do you?"

"Hope springs eternal."

"Well, I've got news for you. Spring has sprung."

Deil made no reply, stretching like a sleepy jungle cat before strolling over to the window where he made the comment, "I suppose Barry drives a fire-engine-red BMW."

Kelly started at his idle words. "How did you know that?"

"Because he just pulled up in front of this building. What did you say?"

"Nothing." She had no intention of repeating her startled expletive.

"Anything I can do to help tidy for our company, dear Watson?" he mockingly offered as she hurriedly cleared the table of their lunch dishes.

"Yes. You can stop calling me dear Watson."

"Shall I just leave it at dear?"

"I know where I'd like to leave you," Kelly muttered.

Deil's expressive voice was laced with conjugal indulgence. "Not now, dear. There's someone at the door."

Deil was opening it before she could make a move to stop him. "Ah, Barry." He reached out a friendly hand to the glowering man. "So glad to see you again."

Kelly had some measure of satisfaction in the brief wince she saw flash across Deil's face. Barry must have been practicing his famous handshake, the one that wrang his opponent's flesh until it felt like a limp rag.

"Still here, Foster?"

"Obviously. Won't you come in and sit down?"

Kelly spotted the telltale ring of white around Barry's mouth, a sure sign that he was furious and trying to hide it. She wasn't expecting his visit, especially since she'd just seen him at the gallery, but she knew better than to say so in front of Deil.

"Yes, come on in, Barry," she invited. "You know your way around." That last statement was made for Deil's benefit, and the gleam in his hazel eyes told her that he was fully cognizant of that fact.

"Kelly tells me you're a journalist." Barry politely murmured the words while draping a proprietal arm around Kelly's shoulders, clearly intent on staking his claim.

Deil was just as intent on making things difficult. "That's right. And I understand that you're in business for yourself."

"I'm an investment advisor," Barry corrected, trying to maintain his good humor.

"Must be fascinating," Deil suggested in a voice that implied otherwise.

Barry gritted his teeth and mused with insulting amazement, "So you're Sally's brother. I didn't know she was English."

"She isn't."

"But you're—"

"No, I'm not," Deil took pleasure in denying.

"Deil's lived in London so long that he just sounds like a native," Kelly explained.

"Well, it was nice of you to look Kelly up while you're in town. How long do you plan on staying?"

"The summer."

Barry's face darkened ominously. "You're not sleeping here, I hope!"

"Of course I'm not sleeping here." Deil waited for Barry's satisfied "Good!" before adding, "I'm sleeping in the bedroom."

CHAPTER THREE

"Sally's bedroom," Kelly quickly clarified before Barry could explode with rage as she suspected he was about to.

"I don't like this setup!" Barry said forcefully.

"I can assure you that Kelly is in no danger from me," Deil blandly replied. "I'm perfectly harmless."

And I'm your grandmother! Kelly immediately thought to herself.

But Barry was nodding with cosmopolitan wisdom, much to her surprise. "Oh, I get it. Well, that's a relief."

"I'm so glad you understand," Deil purred.

What were they talking about? Why had Barry decided that Deil was no longer a threat? Whatever the reason, Barry stopped eyeing Deil as a potential poacher and began addressing him with a condescending air that Kelly found baffling.

"London's a great town," Barry was saying. "Some hot music coming from over there. Boomtown Rats. Bow Wow Wow. Incredible!"

Since Kelly didn't choose to keep up with the new wave of English bands, she didn't know if the latter was a compliment or another rock group.

"Hey," Barry continued. "Since you're a journalist, maybe you've met them?"

"I don't do musical interviews," Deil coolly replied.

Barry didn't stay long after that. Kelly was actually eager for him to leave so she could confront Deil.

"What was that all about?" she demanded the moment the door was closed.

"What was what all about?"

"Why did Barry suddenly decide you were no threat to me?"

"Because I told him so."

"Deil." Her tone warned him that she was rapidly losing patience.

"All right. Luce has decided you're safe because he thinks I prefer boys," Deil bluntly stated.

"He what?" Kelly was shocked.

"He thinks . . ."

"Don't repeat it." She commandingly held up her hand. "I heard you the first time. Where on earth could he have gotten an idea like that?"

"You don't think it's true?" Deil's grin was full of male complacency.

"I'm not stupid."

"Which means Luce is?" was his rhetorical question.

Kelly eyed him reprovingly. "Where did Barry get such an idea?"

"From me."

"Why?" Her voice reflected none of her surprise.

"You told me not to hassle him."

"So you told him . . ."

"I didn't tell him anything," Deil corrected. "You were sitting there the entire time."

"And had no idea what you two were talking about."

"Now you know. Luce is a simple man. To him, harmless means only one thing."

"And what happens when he finds out you're *not* harmless?"

"We'll pass that bridge when we come to it."

"Thanks for the navigational homily," she gibed with a sarcasm that angered Deil.

"What would you have preferred that I do? Tell him I've got a different woman in my bed every night? He'd make your life hell."

"Are you sure you weren't just protecting yourself?"

"From what?" he laughed with disparagement. "That jock?"

"Yes."

Seeing that she was serious, Deil lost both his patience and his temper. "Right!" he bit out. "If that's what you think, we'll just call Luce back and tell him the truth. That I was playing a practical joke on him, that my sexual appetite is as healthy as his is. I don't give a damn what he thinks!"

His next words were muttered almost to himself. "Leave it to a woman to come up with the wrong answer every time." Angrily prowling the perimeter of the living room, Deil stopped before her to hurl the tight-lipped accusation, "Or were you trying to provoke me into proving to you that I don't prefer boys?"

Kelly took just a little too long to answer, and Deil's temper flared completely out of control. He pulled Kelly into his arms, his hazel eyes glaring down at her. A current of excitement jumped between them, spicing the anger with passion. It was an extremely combustible combination.

Currents of desire played along her spinal cord from the nape of her neck to the back of her knees. His body was pressed close to hers, speaking to her in a language all its own. Anger's adrenaline was transformed into passion's arousal.

Kelly saw his eyes widen with the discovery, a new light entering their depths. But before she could put a name to it, a shutter came down. Deil shook his head, as if to clear it of distracting images. "Oh, no, you don't!" he growled, releasing her so fast that she stood swaying. "I'm not going to fall for that one!"

"W—w—what?" Her confusion was reflected in the breathy question.

"Deliberately taunting me into breaking our agreement. Section ten," he recited. "No sexual overtures. Tell your boyfriend whatever you damn well please! I've got work to do!"

After getting off to such an admittedly inauspicious start, living with Deil wasn't as bad as Kelly had expected. Time and proximity provided them with the opportunity of getting to know each other. Naturally there were some adjustments that had to be made on both sides. Kelly, a student of spontaneity, had an artist's bohemian approach to life. Deil was all streamlined organization, a place for everything and everything in its place.

It was this efficiency that led Deil to Kelly's dirty-laundry basket. Since his pile of wash fell shy of a coin-operated machine's full load, he made up the difference with her clothes. She'd been working extra hours at the gallery and then working until late at night at the café. Deil was sure she'd appreciate his generous gesture.

Kelly was home when he returned, laundry basket in hand. "So you decided to brave the laundry," she approved. "Congratulations!"

"All in a day's work." Deil's modest shrug was accom-

41

panied by the grin she'd come to know so well. "I even did some of yours."

"Mine?"

Deil nodded. "I pulled out whatever was in the hamper."

"Oh, no!" she wailed, heading for the bathroom.

He followed her, watching as she peered into the now empty hamper. "What's wrong?"

Kelly made no reply, hurrying back to the living room and the basketful of freshly laundered clothes. Casually folded towels were dislodged as she pawed through the pile with reckless abandon.

"Are you looking for something in particular," Deil inquired with humorous politeness, "or do you have a fetish for clean clothes?"

She pulled out two items, wispy pieces of strung-out lace, and moaned, "What have you done to them?"

"Aren't they supposed to look like that?" he asked in male bewilderment.

"The elastic's all shot, and I just bought these two. Do you know how much bras cost these days?"

"I can't say that I do," he admitted, admiring the way her face was flushed with anger.

"These cost fourteen dollars. Each! It's ridiculous. There's no way the materials could cost that much, and the industry could hardly claim a need for research and development!"

"I'd love to research your development," Deil teased with a devilish gleam.

Kelly experienced the same breathless anticipation she felt whenever he made a suggestive remark. It was an affliction that simultaneously worried and excited her. In fact it was the excitement that worried her!

42

They both tried avoiding physical contact, but in the apartment's relatively close confines some accidental encounters were bound to occur. Even the slightest touch of Deil's hand as he passed her a cup of coffee had the power to incite a response. Kelly knew Deil was aware of it too, aware of it and fighting it. Yet when it came to verbal bantering, neither could resist entering into dangerous waters.

"I'm sure you'd love to research my, umm, development," Kelly archly replied. "But I thought you were a political journalist and not a fashion reporter."

"I was just trying to be helpful. You know, protect myself from a lawsuit for damages."

"I'll agree to drop everything . . ."

"You will?" he exclaimed, rubbing his hands together with lecherous glee.

"I meant the lawsuit," she reprimanded, trying to repress a grin. "On condition . . ."

"I knew there had to be one," Deil sighed.

". . . that you help me pull lead," she finished.

"Pull lead? Is that anything like pumping iron?" he questioned suspiciously.

"Not very." Her grin could be repressed no longer. "I need to stretch a calm of lead."

"Hmm." Deil stroked a nonexistent beard with professorial contemplation. "A calm being a six-foot-long strip of H- or U-shaped lead."

"You do listen!" she marveled in a properly amazed tone.

And so it was that Kelly first brought Deil to see the studio behind Artisans. In contrast to her chaotic approach to cleaning the apartment, here order ruled. Her work area was dominated by two large, sturdy oak tables,

43

each with a metal right angle clamped on. Numerous tools were neatly hanging on a pegboard, and supplies were clearly labeled.

Following Kelly's instructions, Deil took the pair of pliers she handed him and firmly held one end of the calm while her pliers held the other. The lead strip was gently pulled until they felt the telltale snap.

"I can see where this might be a little difficult to do on your own," he commented as they lowered the strip to the floor for future cutting.

"Mmm," she agreed. "I knew you would come in handy one of these days."

Actually she'd come to know a lot about her disturbing roommate. She knew he was addicted to reading a newspaper every day without fail. Kelly teased Deil about his "journal-fix" and cried, "Addict, addict!" while he lounged behind the newsprint. She had no doubt that left to his own devices Deil would read every bit of printed material in the apartment, right down to the rarely used cookbooks. She knew he liked both his coffee and his toast black. Black cherry was his favorite flavor yogurt and ice cream. Sherlock Holmes was his hero.

Deil talked freely about his work, although he never disclosed names or the details about his current book. Kelly was still unaccustomed to having a word processor in the house and made sure that she stayed clear of it, just in case it should throw a temperamental fit and erase something!

A few days later Kelly was the one who felt like she'd had her memory erased. She'd unsuspectingly walked into the kitchen to make herself a peanut butter and jelly sandwich. Pulling out the cutlery drawer, she automatically reached inside for a knife. Instead what she came up with was a handful of potholders. Had she absentmindedly opened the wrong drawer?

Frowning in confusion, she stepped back and looked carefully. No, it was the right drawer, wrong contents! This morning she was positive it had held silverware, as it had every day since she'd moved in.

Two more drawers were pulled out before she discovered the silverware. The same thing happened when she opened a cabinet door and reached inside for a glass. No glasses, but plenty of cans. The dishes weren't where they belonged; in fact, nothing was! There could only be one explanation.

"Deil!"

He was slow in answering her shouted exclamation. "What is it?"

"Have you been messing around in my kitchen?" Her tone was violently indignant.

"Messing around?" He left the word processor and came to stand on the kitchen's threshold. "No . . ."

"Well, *someone's* moved everything around!" she blared.

"I reorganized your kitchen," he went on to say. "That's not messing around."

"In my book it is. Who gave you permission to touch my drawers?" She wished the question unsaid the moment she heard it, knowing the choice of words would leave her wide open for seductive teasing.

Deil's eyes glinted with devilish humor, his voice a soft, sensuous murmur. "Your drawers were irresistible. They were just itching for my attention."

"They were not!" Kelly denied fiercely, disconcerted by the uncomfortably intimate turn their discussion had taken. "From now on, keep your hands—"

"Off your drawers?" he deliberately drawled.

"And cabinets. Otherwise I may be inclined to do a little reorganizing myself, starting with your work table."

Her threat worked, for his expression immediately became wary. "I was trying to make things easier for you to find by putting them in their logical places."

"They were already in their logical places. So you can just put everything back."

They ended up compromising. The silverware, dishes, and glasses were all put back, by both of them. The cans, spices, and cookware were allowed to remain in their new domain.

Kelly spent all day Sunday in the studio trying to complete a large leaded panel that had been commissioned by the owner of a new restaurant. The work couldn't be hurried and took longer than she'd anticipated. Her patience was rewarded by a warm sense of accomplishment as she viewed the final result.

Stained glass was an art form designed to let light in through one side while delighting the viewer on the other. Kelly's strong sense of composition as well as a vibrant feel for color had created an object that was truly a work of art. It was so good, in fact, that she hated parting with it! An identical piece could never be re-created.

She had tried calling Deil to tell him she'd be home late, but the line was continually busy. When Kelly did get home, she discovered why. The phone receiver was hooked into the computer's modem, in a technological conspiracy.

"Where have you been?" Deil demanded before she could express her irritation at having his computer tie up her phone lines.

"I've been at the studio."

"You said you'd be back two hours ago."

"I tried to call, but the lines were busy. Who's Ozzie talking to?" she asked, using Deil's nickname for the word processor.

"London."

Kelly couldn't help it, her mouth dropped open. "London, England?"

"That's where it was last time I looked," was Deil's mocking reply.

"Do you have any idea how much that call is going to cost?"

"Not a clue." Deil cheerfully shrugged. "I let Ma Bell take care of that."

"And who's going to take care of the bill?"

"I will. That was the arrangement, wasn't it?"

"With what you'll be paying Ma Bell you could probably buy this entire building."

"I sincerely doubt that."

Kelly paused in pretended contemplation. "How about the front door?"

"Sounds more realistic," he agreed.

"Why does your computer have to call London? And don't tell me he was homesick," she warned.

"The computer is transferring my revisions for chapter three to my publisher's computer in London."

"Just like that?"

"Just like that."

"Amazing!"

"Thank you," he modestly accepted.

"Not you. Ozzie."

"Ah, do I detect a note of affection there?"

"An artist having affection for a machine?" she scoffed.

"Shhh, he'll hear you."

47

Deil spoke with such conviction that Kelly automatically swung her glance over to check on the computer.

"See?"

"I don't see anything besides an outrageously high phone bill."

"Has anyone ever told you that you worry too much?"

"No, and you'd better not be the first."

"How did your day go?" Deil asked, sensing something was wrong. "Did you finish that piece you were working on?"

"Yes, I did."

"Then why so down?"

Kelly didn't bother denying it; he'd come to know her too well. "Because now I've got to send it out into the cruel world."

"You're sending it out so others can enjoy it. When may I see it?"

"I don't know . . ." This piece was special to Kelly. She hadn't let Deil see it when he'd come to the studio, using the excuse that it wasn't finished yet.

"Kelly," he persevered.

"Tomorrow."

"I'm going to hold you to that."

Hold her? Why did the idea sound so appealing all of a sudden? The day must have been harder than she'd thought. "I think I'll go to bed."

"Is that an invitation?" Deil asked as he always did whenever she mentioned bed. The teasing comment became standard fare, as was Kelly's negative response.

"Nothing doing."

"Oh, I wouldn't say that. 'Night, roomie!"

Kelly didn't realize she'd skipped dinner until she was already in bed. By then she was too comfortable to get up again, so she snuggled down and fell asleep. Hunger pangs woke her in the middle of the night. Slipping on her kimono, she stole into the kitchen. Unlike Deil, she didn't bump into one piece of furniture along the darkened way.

The light from the countertop-model refrigerator she opened was the kitchen's only source of illumination.

"What are you doing?" a male voice demanded, breaking the midnight silence.

Wham! A startled Kelly hit her head on the side of the open door. "How do you manage to sneak up on people so quietly?" she complained, her fingers automatically soothing what was sure to turn into a goose egg. "Are you part Indian, or something?"

"You already know I'm part Scottish."

"It's the other part I'm asking about," she muttered.

"Did you hurt yourself?" Deil asked in concern, noting for the first time the way she was rubbing the corner of her forehead. His lean hand reached out to replace hers, gently feeling for an injury.

Shivers of sensation washed over her. It wasn't fair that the lightest touch of his hand should produce such a wave of emotion! Kelly tried to dispel her spellbound state with levity. "My head has felt better, but I don't think there's any permanent damage done."

"You won't require home brain surgery?" Deil's expression was deliberately crestfallen.

"I'm not going to let your sick jokes ruin my appetite," she determined.

"What appetite was that, my dear Watson?" Even in the semi-darkness Kelly could easily discern his devilish gaze.

"The one for peanut butter."

"I'm crushed!"

"So are the peanuts."

"And you accuse me of sick humor?" Deil peered past her, studying the refrigerator's contents. "What do we have in here? Hmmm. Peanut butter, yogurt, ketchup, avocados." He took each of the items he'd listed, set them on the counter, and flicked on the light switch. "Okay, get some bread and a knife, then we'll be all set."

"We? Didn't you eat dinner?"

"Yes. But that was hours ago. Besides, this is a snack, not a meal. Snacks have a different set of rules."

"They do?" Kelly set out the bread on the flip-down table.

"Sure. They don't have to be healthful, they don't come in courses, and they should be exotic. For example, peanut butter and ketchup sandwiches."

"*Blah!*" The exclamation was accompanied by a grimace of distaste.

"Have you ever tried it?" Deil demanded.

Kelly vigorously shook her head.

"Then what are you going *blah* about? It happens to taste very good."

There was no mistaking her extremely doubtful expression.

"Come on," he coaxed. "Try it; you'll like it."

Kelly closed her eyes and took a tiny bite.

"See? It's not so bad."

"I prefer peanut butter and banana."

Now it was Deil's turn to make a face and Kelly's turn to have him try it. Once started, they found it hard to stop experimenting. Peanut butter and saltines . . . potato chips . . . avocado . . . yogurt . . . apples.

Kelly looked up from the concoction she was creating as Deil reached out, his fingers curling around her wrist. He picked up the butter knife and proceeded to generously

50

spread peanut butter over the side of her index finger. Grasping both ends as if it were a piece of corn on the cob, he lifted her finger to his mouth.

"What do you call this?" *Seduction,* she silently answered herself.

"Finger sandwiches," Deil murmured. "Great English delicacy."

It was great, all right, and it made her feel like a delicious delicacy! As he nibbled on her finger, so the appetizing caress nibbled at her equanimity. Gone was the platonic roommate of the past two weeks. Kelly's five senses were all acutely focused on the awareness of Deil as a man. The magnetic field of attraction was building, holding her in its potent polarity. Kelly felt the indisputable tug of sensual attraction, felt it in disturbing places, felt it not only in her body but also in her heart.

The feeling stayed with her for days, even infiltrating her dreams at night. It was during one such night, when she'd tossed off her covers and was mumbling in her sleep, that Deil heard her as he passed by her room. Cautiously opening the door, he peered into the gloomy interior of her bedroom. It took a moment for his eyes to focus, so he moved closer to the bed.

Without benefit of covers, Kelly's lissome form was tantalizingly draped by a silk nightie. The ruffled elastic neckline was pulled indecently low, the pale blue material a mere breath away from revealing the dusky tip of one breast. Her skin was pale and soft in the darkness, a beckoning temptation.

Deil felt his heart, his desire, and his imagination leap into warp speed. Cursing himself for a fool, he ruthlessly reminded himself that this was his sister's roommate. God knew Sally's last roommate, Fiona, had put him through hell, a hell he had no intention of revisiting!

With brisk efficiency Deil moved to replace the covers Kelly had restlessly tossed off. He'd just finished tucking the sheet around her shoulders when, without warning, her hand shot out to close around his arm with surprising strength. Unprepared for her attack, Deil tumbled forward—across her and the bed!

CHAPTER FOUR

"Damn it!" Deil's curse was only partially muffled by the bedcovers and immediately followed by Kelly's strangled scream. Quickly propping himself upright, Deil automatically clamped his free hand over her mouth, thereby stifling any subsequent screams. "Be quiet!" he growled. "Do you want to wake the entire building? It's only me."

"Deil?" Kelly gasped through his hand.

"Were you expecting someone else?" he dryly inquired, sliding his fingers over the curve of her cheek.

Kelly lifted a hand to her breast, pressing it there as though to prevent her pounding heart from leaping out of her body. "I wasn't expecting anyone. What are you doing in my room?"

"Trying to cover you up!"

"You scared me half to death!" she unsteadily accused, too shaken to appreciate the dishabille of her attire.

Deil had the opposite problem; his appreciation was too strong, too deep, and it shook him. Kelly's body was soft and yielding beneath the sheet's ineffectual barrier. Sprawled as he was, half across her, he could feel each breath she drew. The rapid rise and fall of her breasts silently spoke of her alarmed state. Well meaning though his intentions may have been, he had obviously frightened her.

In an attempt to make amends, Deil reached out to touch her hand, the one closest to him, which happened to be pressed to her heart. "I'm sorry," he murmured softly. "I didn't mean to scare you."

His hand lay atop hers, a small reminder of the way his body lay atop hers. Not that Kelly needed reminding. This thrill, this running sensation of excitement was a feeling only Deil could provoke.

Thinking only to remove herself from the incendiary danger of his touch, Kelly abruptly slipped her hand away. But that left his hand pressed to her now galloping heart.

Her dazed eyes widened at the unintentional caress, her breast blossoming in his palm. Skin reacted to bare skin, overriding the dictates of caution. Seemingly of their own volition, his fingers moved over her burgeoning form.

Kelly was spellbound by the intricate magic of his caress. She voiced no protest, lodged no complaint. Her eyes, formerly heavy with sleep, became slumberous with passion. Nerve endings were alive to sensation as his hand stroked its way to a taut, dusky peak.

Without saying a word Deil unhurriedly lowered his head to hers. She felt the soft puff of his breath before the lingering presence of his lips. This was their first kiss, and it carried some of the tentativeness of such a caress, the seeking of knowledge, the adjusting of shape and form. Yet there was an underlying rightness that permeated throughout.

The warm pressure of his mouth deepened as he tasted her instinctive response. Lips parted, tongues darted, and flames started! Kelly's toes curled in languid delight, her arms encircling Deil's waist, her hands climbing up his back.

Flashes of her favorite children's fairy tale, "The Three Bears," came to mind. Not too heavy, not too tall; like the baby bear's porridge, Deil was just right! Their bodies seemed specifically designed to fit together in such a delectable manner, her softness conforming to his hardness, his virility responding to her warmth.

It was a reciprocal embrace, with both parties sharing in the discoveries. Her sensitized fingertips delighted in the texture of his skin while his lips registered the pounding pulse at the base of her neck.

Caught up in her own exploration of Deil's powerful body, Kelly was unaware that the hem of her nightgown was gradually inching up. In fact, she was unaware of anything outside of the realm of pleasure he'd transported her to! As Deil surveyed the bared line of her leg, her murmurs of pleasure prompted him to linger along the back of her knee. There his questing fingers detected a slight alteration in the creamy smoothness of her skin. Was it . . . a scar?

"What happened?" The question was murmured against her lips as his finger lightly continued its investigation.

Kelly stiffened, the change in her immediately apparent. She hadn't thought about David or the accident in months. With her defenses down, she murmured the name in an exhalation of pain. "David."

The name had a disastrous affect on Deil. "Is that whom you were expecting, whom you thought you were tumbling into your bed?" He jackknifed away from her, his feet hitting the hardwood floor with a resounding thump.

Kelly vainly tried to explain. "I didn't . . . That's not—"

"Save your breath." Deil fiercely cut her off, slamming out of her room.

Kelly got very little sleep for the remainder of the night. The memory of Deil's caresses, the thought of his warm body pressed against hers became a mental thorn that chafed and pierced her fatigue. At eight thirty the next morning the bathroom mirror threw back the reflection of her disturbed weariness. Her tan seemed washed out, her eyes darkly shadowed. The shirt and pants she'd chosen, in complimentary shades of plum, were usual morale boosters. The narrow-cuffed trousers accentuated the length of her legs and the striped V-neck shirt clung without being snug. So why did she feel like a damp mop?

Kelly nearly groaned aloud when she found Deil sitting in the living room, obviously intent on speaking to her before she left for the gallery. Perhaps speaking was a mild way of putting it, actually he looked more prepared for a showdown! Kelly squared her shoulders and warily gathered her defenses.

"Good morning," she politely greeted him.

"No, it isn't," was his surly contradiction.

"Whatever you say." She shrugged, moving into the kitchen.

"I have a lot to say. To you."

"And very little time in which to say it." Kelly pointed to the teapot-shaped kitchen clock. "I have to be at the gallery in twenty minutes and it takes me at least ten minutes to walk there."

"Then I suggest you sit down so we can get started."

Kelly sipped at a glass of orange juice before saying, "I'll stand, thank you."

"Fine. Since I know you're in a hurry, I'll be blunt. I

56

don't know how you get your kicks, but last night was not my idea of a fun time."

Now was the time to explain. "Deil, about last night . . ."

But he refused to hear her. "I'd rather not rehash it, if you don't mind. It isn't my intention to hold a postmortem."

"Then what is your intention?"

"To make it clear that I don't want a repeat of last night. The way I see it, we're stuck with each other for the next nine weeks. I suggest we both look elsewhere for sexual gratification. I can sure as hell tell you that I won't be lured into your bedroom again!"

"Lured!" she echoed in astonishment. "You seem to have a few things backward. I was sound asleep. You were the one who waltzed into my room and fell onto my bed. No invitation was ever issued to you. Unless Sally offered you the use of her roommate as well as her apartment!" Kelly waspishly finished.

Deil's face looked uncompromising, the proverbial wooden Indian. "You can't know my sister very well if you think she'd even consider that." His tone was equally wooden.

"I'm sorry."

Deil ruined her apology by saying, "So you should be."

"And so should you be," she shot back.

"Oh, I'm sorry all right," Deil derisively acknowledged. "Sorry I ever bothered checking on you last night!"

"Then make sure you don't ever bother checking again!" Kelly flared with an anger befitting her Irish heritage.

"You need have no fear on that account," was his grim assurance.

"Fine. I'm so glad we've cleared the air by having this little chat."

Of course the air wasn't cleared at all; it was full of tension for the next two days. Deil had to work in the apartment and Kelly refused to be chased out of her home, so the stalemate continued. Neither wanted to be the first to break down.

"Look, can't we at least be civilized about this?" Deil evenly inquired on the third day of their hostilities.

"Oh, by all means, let's be civilized," Kelly mocked.

"You're impossible!"

"You should know," she returned sweetly.

"Why? Because I live with you?"

"No, because you've perfected being impossible to a fine art!"

"Coming from an artist, I'll take that as a compliment. And speaking of artists, I stopped by that new restaurant last night and saw your panel. I never did get to see it at the studio," he reminded her. "You're very talented."

Kelly searched for some sign of sarcasm, but found none. His tone and expression were both marked with sincerity. "Thank you."

"When I complimented the owner on his great taste in stained glass, he told me you're going to be showing at the Snowmass Art Fair."

"That's right. It's this weekend."

"How's the work going?"

"Not very well," she grimaced. "How about you?"

"Same here." Deil sounded disgusted.

Kelly knew the feeling, the frustration of not having the creative juices flowing the way they should. She also knew of a cure. But should she suggest it, or would Deil get the wrong impression yet again? Always a creature of impulse, she decided on the spur of the moment that she'd make the suggestion. Deil could take it or leave it!

"It's a beautiful day. What do you think of playing hooky this afternoon and going out to Maroon Bells?"

"You and I?"

"Yes."

"Why?"

"Because you're the one with the car." Kelly didn't own one. "But you don't have to worry," she mockingly assured him. "I promise not to attack you while you're driving! Or at any other time!"

Deil grinned at her tart rejoinder. "Shall we call it a truce for the afternoon?"

"Deal," she agreed.

"What?"

"What do you mean what?" Kelly frowned in bewilderment.

"You said my name."

"No, I was agreeing to a truce. D-e-a-l," she spelled out.

"Well, then, are you ready to go?" he questioned.

"No. I have to go change. I'll be back in a second."

"That's all right," he graciously allowed. "I won't time you!"

Kelly was back in ten minutes wearing jeans and a checked flannel shirt over a navy T-shirt. In her hand she carried a bright orange rucksack. "All set," she announced.

"This is the last week you're allowed to drive up to Maroon Bells during the day," she told him as they headed west on Highway 82, out of town. "From the beginning of July through Labor Day the road is closed to cars. Then you have to use the shuttle bus service that the park service provides."

"Why's that?"

"Because each year thousands of people come to see Maroon Bells. It's one of the most photographed natural sites in America. Turn left here," she paused to instruct. "Then take the fork to the right." Kelly waited until they'd passed the park official's gatehouse before continuing with her explanation. "The fumes from all those cars were killing the aspen trees. The ecological balance is very delicate. You can still see several stands of dead aspens." She pointed out the window.

"I'm surprised you let me drive."

"Ordinarily I would've made you take the shuttle too. It's running now, but isn't mandatory."

"You said ordinarily?"

"Mmm. I wanted to stop on the way back; there's a pull-off with a beautiful view of the mountains. I've been very good and haven't visited it once this year. I thought today I'd treat myself, and you, to that special view."

"I'm honored."

"So you should be," she teased in return.

There were several minutes of companionable silence before Deil asked, "Why do so many aspens die all at once? I've seen several groups, but rarely one unhealthy tree on its own."

"That's because aspens grow in families, with interwoven root systems. These families are known as clones. And no clone jokes, please."

Deil looked insulted. "I'll have you know that I'm a journalist, not a stand-up comic!"

"There are times when I wonder."

"Tell me some more about the aspens," he instructed, slowing to drive across the metal bars of a cattle guard.

"Their normal life span is similar to that of a human being's."

"You almost make them sound human."

Kelly smiled to herself. She did feel that way about the aspens. There was something special about them, a delicate beauty she admired. During the summer their long-stemmed leaves waved at the slightest breeze, turning each tree into a mass of rippling verdant hands. In the fall those same leaves turned brilliant shades of orange and gold, their autumn colors blazing across the hillsides.

After parking the car at the lower lot, they followed the directional walking signs marked MAROON LAKE.

"Am I seeing things, or are these side mountains red?" Deil questioned in disbelief.

"You're not seeing things. The iron ore deposits give them that intense red color."

"It certainly makes for a striking combination against that blue sky."

Although they had caught glimpses of Maroon Bell's twin peaks from the road during the drive up, it couldn't compare to the sight before them now. The lake was crystal clear with a vibrant color only glacier water has. It glistened in the sunlight, a jewel hanging from the mountains' base.

"Pretty impressive, hmmm?" she prompted.

"Very," he agreed.

"Teddy Roosevelt once said of Colorado that the scenery bankrupts the English language."

They followed the main route around the lake until they came to a fork in the path. Kelly chose the less traveled of the two. Now, as they walked along, there were no backpackers passing them, no excited children racing around them, no harried parents trudging behind them.

Instead, a peaceful silence encompassed them, and the only sounds heard were those of nature. Icy creeks tumbled down the mountains, joining forces to feed the lake. A sea of quaking aspens rustled in the gentle breeze. The air was decidedly cool and patches of snow could still be found remarkably close by. The generous amount of snow still covering the mountains led Deil to ask about the area's annual snowfall.

"Last year they had about two hundred inches up here. There could still be more."

"More?"

"Sure. It's not at all unusual to have snow squalls up on the mountains throughout the summer months. For all that matter, even back in Aspen we've been known to get a few inches dumped on us in June. You've been lucky so far."

"I guess I have been," Deil was forced to agree. Then, noting an aspen tree behind them, he said, "I see some romantic fools have carved entwining initials to symbolize their undying love."

"There's nothing romantic about killing a tree," Kelly fiercely countered. "And carving initials on an aspen's sensitive bark does just that!"

"So much for undying love."

Kelly made no reply to his droll comment, perched as she was atop a huge boulder, her knees bent in the classic pose of a rockbound mermaid. Her legs were delightfully shown off by a pair of stretch jeans. The rucksack she'd brought along had been stuffed with the pink shetland sweater and maroon down vest she was now wearing.

A decided bite in the air prompted Deil to tug on the Irish wool sweater that was casually tied around his shoulders. His dark wavy hair was ruffled in the process, lending him an endearingly boyish appeal. The rumpled strands were smoothed away from his eyes by his impatient fingers. He then joined Kelly on her perch, where they sat in amiable tranquility.

Kelly was the one who finally broke the silence. "I always feel better when I come up here. The scenery revitalizes me."

"I can see why," Deil quietly replied. "It's spectacular."

Kelly nodded dreamily, her thoughts on the majesty of the mountains. "There's enough space up here."

"Didn't you tell me that there are ninety-five thousand acres of wilderness? That should be space enough for anyone."

"There speaks a city lad," Kelly mocked.

"Where did you live B.A.?"

"B.A.?"

"Before Aspen."

"Upstate New York," she confessed.

"So under this Western façade"—his fingers teasingly flicked her denims—"you're just an Eastern tenderfoot, same as me."

Kelly had learned from Sally that both she and her brother grew up in Connecticut. Their father was a prominent attorney in the field of international law.

"Was your father upset that you didn't follow in his legal footsteps?" she found herself asking.

"No, not at all. Since my writing leans toward political analysis, we share a number of similar interests."

"Don't you find it a shock to be here in the wilderness after spending so much time in London?"

"Not as big a shock as living with you has been!"

His statement broke their temporary truce. Without a word, Kelly hopped off the boulder, swept up her rucksack, and stalked off. Swearing under his breath, Deil quickly followed. It didn't take him long to catch up with her, but the pugnacious angle of her chin told him that he wouldn't have such an easy time mending broken fences.

"Kelly, wait a minute! Let me explain."

"Why should I?" she countered, not breaking her stride. "You wouldn't let me explain the other night."

Deil's expression tightened with anger as he hiked beside her. "No explanations were necessary."

"As are none now. Your words were perfectly clear. Let me remind you that no one is forcing you to stay at the apartment. You're free to leave at any time." Her inflection silently added, *The sooner, the better.*

Their return to the parking lot was marked with a hostile silence. Angered by what he perceived to be typical female stubbornness, Deil walked past a waiting shuttle bus without really seeing it. As soon as he realized that his angry strides had left Kelly behind, he paused, watching in disbelief as she walked into the bus instead of around it! The vehicle's doors folded shut and the bus took off before Deil could make a move to stop it.

Kelly settled into the first free seat, too furious to be bothered by the prospect of Deil's reaction. So living with her was a shock, was it? Then her latest performance should come as no surprise to him. She mutinously stared out the window, which was where her peace of mind had gone. Right out the window!

By the time Deil got to his rented subcompact, there was no way he could safely catch up with the shuttle. *Well done, Foster,* he silently congratulated himself. *You really blew that one!*

The late afternoon and early evening found them both

at their respective places of work, Deil at the word processor and Kelly at the studio. Bonnie seemed surprised to see her friend.

"I didn't know you were planning on using the studio today."

"Will it interfere with your plans?"

"Not at all. I enjoy the company. We haven't had much time to talk. How're things going with you?"

"Fine," Kelly lied.

"Are you all set for this weekend's art fair?"

"That's what I'm doing tonight. There are still a few pieces that need leading up and finishing."

"How's your English deal?" Bonnie had taken to referring to Deil that way ever since she'd first heard about him.

Kelly muttered a stream of mostly unintelligible insults.

"I got 'stubborn' and 'pig-headed,' but I'm afraid I missed the rest," Bonnie teasingly apologized.

"He's impossible!"

"So you've told me. I still say you should be pleased that he's so organized. Even you had to admit that it's been easier to find things since he rearranged your kitchen cabinets! What's the problem this time?"

Kelly didn't know how to explain without going into embarrassing details about that night in her bedroom. This time the problem wasn't a matter of Deil's organizational skill, but rather his sex appeal! "I'd rather not talk about it."

"Okay," Bonnie easily agreed. "How did Aspen's newest restaurateur like his commissioned work of art?"

"He liked it fine. Invited me to come visit it whenever I wanted to."

It took the utmost self-discipline for Kelly to curb her thoughts and concentrate on her work. All aspects of her craft required absolute accuracy, and therefore absolute concentration. At ten thirty she carefully wrapped the last multicolored pane in tissue paper before placing it into the protected confines of a transit box. Since Bonnie was also displaying in the art fair, she had offered to provide the transportation.

Saturday's weather was perfect and the show drew a good crowd. Kelly was pleased with the brisk sales. By afternoon she'd even had a buyer for one of her more expensive Tiffany-style lamps as well as several inlaid mirrors. She was sitting in her deck chair, a jaunty visor cap shielding her face from the bright sunlight while a pair of sunglasses protected her eyes from the glare, when she sensed someone's presence beside her.

Deil stood there, and even more surprising, he was alone. He looked too good for comfort in his jeans and a light blue polo shirt. Where was his rumpled business suit? Where was the pallor he'd had when he'd first arrived at her apartment? Where was her self-control?

"What happened to Sandy and Tami?" she questioned, naming the two women he'd been going out with. "Aren't they art lovers?"

"I don't know what kind of lovers they are. At least not yet."

The male complacency of his expression made Kelly lose her temper. "Saving yourself for marriage, are you?" she rudely sniped.

Instead of getting angry as she expected, Deil had the effrontery to laugh at the ludicrousness of such a sugges-

66

tion. "There speaks a frustrated roommate. Jealous, my dear Watson?"

"How's your English . . ." Bonnie's teasing question trailed off the moment she spied the man standing next to Kelly.

"My English is fine," Deil grinned. "In fact, I've been told that I speak the language like a native." The claim was delivered with his best British accent.

"I'm Bonnie Cherinsky," she introduced herself, thrusting out a capable hand. "You must be Sally's brother."

"And you must be Aspen's most talented potter."

"Kelly didn't tell me you were such an accomplished flatterer."

"What did she tell you?"

"That you're Sally's brother."

"Not only are you talented, but you're also diplomatic!" Deil complimented Bonnie with exaggerated flair.

Bonnie's eyes flashed Kelly a silent, but eloquent, message. *Snap this one up!* Aloud she said, "I've got to get back to my M&M's." With a cheerful wave she drifted away.

"Her M&M's?" Deil turned to ask Kelly. "Is she a candy addict?"

"No, she's a devoted mother. The M&M's she was referring to are Magda and Mircha, her two-month-old twins."

"Is her husband an artist too?"

"Oh, Ivan's into leather." Kelly delighted in the momentary look of shock that Deil wasn't quite able to hide, even though his expression immediately resumed its former blandness.

"Hand-tooled leather," she continued. "Belts, boots, wallets—that sort of thing."

67

"You, my dear Watson, have an acerbic sense of humor."

"And that bothers you," was her immediate presumption.

"Mmm, it bothers me all right, but not in the way it's meant to. I find it very stimulating . . . in every sense of the word." Deil's accompanying look was as warm as the summer sun.

In the past Kelly had often used her sharp sense of humor as a deflating weapon on those men who'd been too amorous. Was this supposed to be poetic justice, then? That she was living with a roommate who found her humor sexy instead of dampening!

"Wrap two dozen of those and have them sent to my country estate in Sussex," Deil suddenly intoned, his accent one of lordly largess. He strode away with aristocratic hauteur, leaving behind one stymied roommate and several open-mouthed bystanders.

"Do you suppose he's really a lord, Martha?" one elderly man was overheard to say.

All the next day Kelly anticipated another appearance by Deil. She hadn't seen him last night, had only heard him come in well after her own late arrival. The organizers of the art and craft show had set up an impromptu barbecue for the participants. Bonnie had made a beeline straight for Kelly, intent on stating her favorable first impression of Deil. "How can you complain about living with such a gorgeous hunk?"

Kelly played dumb. "Are you talking about Deil?"

"Of course I'm talking about Deil. What other gorgeous hunk are you living with?"

68

"I wouldn't exactly describe him as a hunk," Kelly falsely protested.

"Are you kidding? His body is perfectly proportioned, if a little on the slim side. It seems criminal to waste that healthy head of hair on a mere male. Then there's that velvety voice and that delicious accent. His features are strong and memorable without any of Barry's blandness." Bonnie had never liked Barry, and had never hidden the fact.

"Don't you think Ivan would be jealous if he heard you talking about another man like this?" Kelly teased in an attempt to change the subject.

"Come on. Just because I'm married, it doesn't mean I'm dead! And you'd have to be a zombie not to notice your English deal's bedroom eyes. Ivan's got them too; that's why I'm such an expert!"

Kelly had to laugh at Bonnie's self-satisfied expression.

"I'm surprised Barry hasn't thrown a tantrum about the arrangement," Bonnie continued.

"Deil assured Barry that I was safe with him." Kelly omitted to mention the mind game Deil had played on Barry.

"Barry believed you're safe with Deil?" Bonnie was incredulous.

"He's having his doubts now." *And so am I,* Kelly silently added. No matter how hard she tried, she couldn't forget that night Deil had come into her room. The sensual scene replayed itself time and time again.

Since Deil hadn't put in an appearance at Sunday's art show, Kelly assumed he must be spending the day with one of his girl friends. She was surprised to find him at the apartment when she returned a little after five. At least she assumed it was Deil singing off-key in the shower. She knew of no one else who dah-dah-dahed their way through "God Save the Queen!"

Kelly was on her way to her rocking chair, a plateful of cold quiche in hand, when she heard Deil's unmistakable curse. Fearing he'd hurt himself, she hurried to the hallway. The bathroom was deserted, but the trail of wet footprints led to Sally's room. She gingerly knocked on the half-open door, uncertain of his state of dress, or undress. What a change from the first day he'd arrived, when she'd dared him to undress before her. Kelly's knock made the door swing open to reveal Deil, dressed in a pair of dark trousers and white shirt, on all fours.

"Don't move!" he barked.

His tone of voice, that of a man who'd just sighted a deadly rattler, stopped Kelly in her tracks. "What's wrong?"

"I've dropped my contact," he impatiently explained, scouring the plush carpet with his hands.

"You wear contacts?"

"No, I keep them as pets!" Deil sarcastically retorted.

"Then you should train them to come when you whistle. You know how to whistle, don't you, Deil?" Kelly lowered her voice to a husky Lauren Bacall imitation. "You just put your lips together and blow."

"Would you mind cutting the vaudeville and getting down here to help me find my damn lens?"

Kelly had to grin at his impatience. "I'd be delighted." She gracefully dropped to her knees and joined in the search. It didn't take her long to sight the tiny circle of plastic. "There it is!"

"Where?"

"Over there!" Kelly put out a directional hand at the same time Deil, whose depth perception wasn't very good without his contacts, turned toward her. Her hand hit his arm in precisely the right manner to make the supporting limb fold at the elbow. A second later they were both sprawled full-length on the plush carpet.

CHAPTER FIVE

"Your knocking me off-balance like this is fast becoming a habit!" Deil growled against her throat.

Kelly tried to wriggle free, a mistake, for it brought her body more fully into contact with the male length of his. She was trapped between the plush softness of the carpet beneath her and the overwhelming masculinity above her. Yet his was a seductive trap, luring her ever deeper into its alluring snare.

With a muffled groan Deil shifted slightly, so that his lips could appraise the pure line of her jaw. The mere feel of his warm mouth on her skin was enough to melt away all thought of resistance. Her arms reached up to curve around the nape of his neck, urging him closer. She felt an overwhelming need to have him kiss her, a need he took his time in satisfying.

First there was the teasing survey of the entire circumference of her mouth. No curve was left untouched. "You taste good . . ." His compliment was murmured against the soft flesh of her lower lip. "Like . . . ?" Deil paused to once more sample the moist delicacy, the flavor of her lip gloss forgotten in the face of more pleasurable pastimes.

Like, want, need . . . The chain of word associations

clamored around Kelly's brain until she could no longer think straight, could no longer think at all, just feel. And, God, it felt good, it felt right to be kissing him.

Deil turned the caress into outright seduction, easing to a gossamer light brushing of lips. The tantalizing stroking back and forth continued until tremors of delight were dancing up and down Kelly's spine in glorious expectation. At the apex of her anticipation his roving mouth settled on hers, the firm pressure an invitation rather than a demand. It was an invitation Kelly unreservedly accepted, parting her lips and bidding him inside.

Deil's tongue paused at the pearly gates of her teeth, gliding over them with warm acknowledgment. Then Kelly could wait no longer and her own tongue hastened to join his in erotic play. Their mouths melded together, the dark interior becoming an oral playground, the likes of which Kelly had never imagined. One kiss became two, two became four, the caresses rapidly escalating. It was as if their bodies had been designed for each other, as if their lips had feasted together on many such sensual banquets.

Soft murmurs of pleasure made their way to the surface —his inaudible growls, hers lilting purrs. The expenditure of oxygen left Kelly's mind hazy and increased the trembling in her limbs. Deil slowly lifted his mouth from hers, sucking in cool drafts of air. She could feel his inhalation and exhalation, feel the freshness of his breath fanning her burning cheeks. She could also hear a ringing in her ears.

They had only been kissing, yet their involvement had been so deep that it took them several moments to regain some measure of composure. Meanwhile the phone rang on, its shrill call demanding attention.

Deil untangled himself and attempted to rise, but Kelly

stopped him with the reminder, "Your contact. It's there by the foot of the bed."

He reached out to pick up the recalcitrant lens before swiftly standing. Kelly noted the disturbed huskiness of his voice as he answered the phone beside the bed. The call was for him. One of his admiring legions, no doubt. Kelly scrambled to her feet with more speed than grace. There were times when retreat was the better part of valor, and this was definitely one of them!

She locked herself in her own room, feeling juvenile for doing so, yet intent on avoiding seeing Deil again. She was successful; the soft click of the front door proclaimed his departure. Of course, further meetings were inevitable, but by then Kelly resolved to have her wayward emotions under control.

Their next meeting came as Kelly prepared a late breakfast the next morning. It was Monday, and she didn't have to work at the gallery, so she'd slept late. The tension was tangible from the moment Deil stepped into the small kitchen.

He got right to the point. "I think we should talk."

Kelly had two options: she could feign ignorance or don a cloak of cool compliance. She chose the latter. "I agree."

Gathering her coffee cup and a day-old croissant, Kelly regally swept into the living room. Deil waited until she was comfortably seated in her customary rocking chair before speaking.

"We've obviously got a problem on our hands."

The mere mention of the word *hands* forcibly brought to mind the delectable pleasure his caressing hands had incited. In her mind's eye she could still picture them touching her, in places . . . *Stop it!* she tersely ordered herself.

"Let's try and look at this objectively, shall we?" Deil continued as if he were discussing the weather.

Was this the same man who'd kissed her almost senseless last night on the bedroom floor? How was she supposed to shut off her thoughts and feelings? But if Deil could do it, so could she. "By all means, let's be objective," she agreed with deceptive blandness, taking a sip of coffee for good measure.

Deil swiftly checked her expression for signs of sarcasm, but could discern nothing behind her mask of outward calm. "Here's the situation as I see it. Because of our living together, our constant proximity has nurtured a growing attraction between us."

"It could happen to anyone." Kelly's tone was one of logical justification.

"Right." However, Deil didn't look as though there was much going right at the moment. "Now we have to come up with some way of alleviating the potential danger caused by our living arrangements. Any suggestions?"

"That you move out," Kelly promptly replied.

"You know I can't afford to do that."

"And I can't afford   " She bit her tongue in the nick of time.

"What?" he prompted.

"Never mind." She dismissed the question with an airy wave of her hand that dropped croissant crumbs on the floor. "So we're agreed that this attraction is a temporary phenomenon, artificially fostered by our living together as roommates, and nurtured by the fact that we see so much of each other in the course of a day?"

Deil nodded, albeit somewhat reluctantly.

"Then the obvious thing to do is see less of each other," was her decision.

"How do you propose we do that?"

"Focus on our lives outside the apartment." Kelly was extremely proud of the dispassionate evenness of her voice. "Sales are up at the gallery, and I'll probably be spending more days there as well as in the studio. Evenings I'll either be working at the coffee house or going out with Barry."

"That's still on?"

"I think it would be best if we didn't delve into each other's private lives," she gently reprimanded Deil. "You go your way, and I'll go mine."

"Fine." Deil's shrug was a study of nonchalance. "That's the most sensible thing to do."

"Then it's agreed?"

"Absolutely."

Deil's dating increased until Kelly could no longer keep track of the fashionable names. It seemed whenever the phone rang it was a husky feminine voice asking for Deil. The sheer volume of calls had forced Kelly to buy a package of self-adhesive notepaper, which she stuck to the outside of Deil's bedroom door!

How Deil still found the time to write and do his share of the chores, she'd never know. Yet the garbage was always taken out, his laundry taken care of. The idea did occur to her that he might be having one of his numerous girl friends doing the work, but she never saw any proof of that.

With the Fourth of July weekend coming up, Kelly found plenty to keep herself occupied. Barry planned on having a huge bash to celebrate Independence Day. Kelly had accepted his invitation several weeks before, but was now anticipating the event with something less than eagerness.

When Bonnie had invited her to a family picnic for the afternoon of the Fourth, she had accepted. Bonnie and her husband owned a sprawling place a few miles west of town. Kelly was grateful for an excuse to get away from the apartment, away from Aspen itself for that matter. The town went crazy on the Fourth, seeing the holiday as an excuse for a series of free-for-all water-balloon fights and other general merrymaking.

"What's new with your English deal?" Bonnie wanted to know after thanking Kelly for the bowl of fresh fruit salad she'd brought.

"I don't see enough of him to know."

"How much is enough?" Bonnie pressed with deliberately lurid interest.

"Are all potters as bad as you are?" Kelly demanded in exasperation.

"No, some are even worse!"

"It's working with all that wet clay that does it," Kelly decided.

"Don't give me that. Stained glass is also a very tactile art."

They bickered about their respective artistic fields of endeavor for several more minutes, but Bonnie soon returned to the subject of Deil.

"Your roommate gave my husband a very strange look at the Snowmass show. I wonder why that was?"

"Might have been because I told him Ivan was into leather."

"Kelly Watson! What a thing to say," Bonnie reprimanded in pseudo-shocked tones. The effect was ruined by a giggled, "I wish I could've seen Deil's face."

"It was priceless," Kelly agreed with a giggle of her own. "Deil tried to recover, but he wasn't fast enough."

"Your sense of humor is going to get you into trouble one of these days," Bonnie warned.

"It makes life much more interesting, more appealing."

"Your life's not that appealing on its own?"

"There are . . . complications," Kelly finally admitted. "You've no idea what it's like having a male roommate."

"What would you call Ivan?"

"He's a husband," Kelly dismissed. "That's different."

"I'm sure he'd be thrilled to have you say so."

Kelly tried to explain. "Ivan's your best friend. It's all right to walk around in old clothes if you want to, or leave your hair unbrushed if you feel like it."

"Deil makes you brush your hair?"

"His presence makes me feel that I can never lower my guard. It didn't matter if Sally saw me looking like a slob."

"But it does matter if Deil sees you looking like a slob?"

"Yes!" Kelly burst out.

"Sounds to me like you're discovering Deil Foster is the hunk I told you he was," Bonnie diagnosed. "And you're definitely interested."

"I won't deny that there's a certain element of mutual attraction." Kelly shrugged. "It's only natural given the circumstances. We're both human, and sexual awareness is a very strong human emotion."

"So what's the problem? You're both over twenty-one."

"Neither one of us wants to get involved."

"You're living together," Bonnie reminded her. "That's already involved."

"You know what I mean."

"No, I don't," Bonnie denied with exaggerated innocence. "Why not tell me about it?"

"As a mother of twins you're trying to tell me you don't know the facts of life?"

Bonnie grinned. "I found them . . ."

"Don't give me that story about how you found your M&M's in the cabbage patch," Kelly sternly instructed, unaware that Bonnie's husband had joined them.

"Actually, it was a radish patch," Ivan inserted with a straight face.

Kelly returned to her apartment later that afternoon in good spirits, having enjoyed the time spent with her friends. She still wasn't looking forward to Barry's party, but was determined to have a good time anyway. She was on her way to take a shower, kimono firmly wrapped around her otherwise naked body, when she discovered that the bathroom was already occupied. Realizing that time was of the essence, and that Deil loved taking long hot showers, Kelly banged on the door and demanded, "How long are you going to be?"

Kelly put her head to the thick wooden door so that she could hear his answer, but there was no reply. Instead, Deil flung open the door and caught a startled Kelly in his arms. He was dripping wet, only a bath towel providing a semblance of modesty.

"Ah, it's the Kamikaze Kimono, I see!" That wasn't all he could see. The front of her robe had gapped to generously reveal the soft slopes of her breasts.

Deil's hands tightened their hold on Kelly's shoulders, whether to pull her closer or push her away she didn't know and wasn't able to discover because she suddenly realized that the bath towel he'd hurriedly wrapped around his waist was slipping. Deil must have realized it too, for they both reached for the terry-cloth covering at the same time. Kelly jerked away as though burned, her fingers tingling from the momentary contact with his firm masculine flesh.

"I'll come back later," she croaked, turning tail and leaving.

An hour later they were both fully clothed and once more in full control of their heightened emotions, or at least giving a fair imitation of being so. Kelly kept stealing surreptitious glances at Deil, watching him as he walked over to pour himself a drink. Why was it that Barry, who spent a mint on his collection of designer jeans, couldn't wear them with the same style that Deil lent to a simple pair of Levis?

Aspen was full of blue-jeaned young men, from dusty cowboy denims to monogrammed extravagances. Yet not once had Kelly ever felt the surge of attraction she felt now, looking at Deil. A black velvet jacket added the proper touch of classy elegance, and his pale blue shirt had a dark red silk tie neatly knotted beneath the collar.

Kelly was not the only one stealing looks. Deil's attention was riveted on her and it took all his willpower to refrain from outright staring. The semi-sheer Indian cotton of Kelly's dress invited speculation as to its diaphanousness, the vivid printed design a perfect foil for her dark hair. Her green eyes, surely the source of her Irish name, glowed in a perfectly made-up face. Soft mauve lips were outlined with a lip pencil, their glossy fullness tempting him to . . . *Forget it, Foster,* was his firm self-instruction.

Deil hid his disturbed state behind cool conversation. "You're going out this evening?"

"Obviously," Kelly replied, using one of his favorite phrases.

"Good. I'd hate to think of anyone being alone on the Fourth of July."

"You're so noble," she gibed.

Deil turned to face her, another glass of whiskey in hand. "Aren't I, though."

"Please feel free to use the apartment this evening," she offered, her tone regally distant.

"Why, thank you." The tilt of his head was a mocking acknowledgment, as was the silent toast he offered her. "I'll do that. When will you be back?"

"No way of telling."

Deil's hazel eyes narrowed suspiciously. "What do you mean?"

"Barry's parties have a habit of lasting all night. So don't bother waiting up for me."

"I wouldn't think of it." Although his inflection was smooth, he looked like he'd just swallowed something bitter.

Kelly decided the whiskey must not be to his taste. She turned as if to leave, disappointed that he had made no mention of her dress. Especially since this was the first time he'd seen her in one!

As if reading her mind, Deil spoke. "Don't you think that dress is a little . . ." He paused for a moment, searching for a suitable word, one that wouldn't reveal his jealous interest.

"A little what?" Kelly belligerently inquired.

". . . cool for this evening?" he compromised, recognizing the angry fire in her kelly-green eyes.

"If I get cold, I'll have Barry to warm me."

"I'm sure you will."

"So who's the lucky girl tonight?" she asked, not bothering to look up from checking her tiny evening bag for her keys.

"Tara."

"Tell Cara I said hi."

"It's Tara."

Kelly shrugged her disinterest. "Whatever."

"I'll be sure and give Tara your regards." His polite assurance was laced with sarcasm.

"Fine. I'll be on my way then."

"I could give you a lift."

I'm sure you could, was Kelly's immediate thought, as she remembered the powerful virility of Deil's body from their earlier encounter in the bathroom. Aloud she said, "No, thank you. Barry is picking me up." As if on cue, the sound of a car's horn drifted up to them.

"Your carriage has arrived, Cinderella," Deil mockingly informed her.

She ignored him, heading for the door. She was actually crossing the threshold when he laid a compelling hand on her arm.

"Kelly, don't stay out all night." Were his husky words a request, a plea, an order, or a demand? She looked up, hoping to find the answer in his eyes. But their eye contact was as volatile as their physical contact, setting the same sensual chain reaction into motion. The warmth of his gaze carried an indecipherable message that passed between them and cast its own spell.

That spell was broken by another impatient hoot of Barry's BMW's horn. Deil released her arm and Kelly hurried down the outside staircase.

Two hours later the party was in full swing and Kelly had a splitting headache. The combination of heavy smoke and blaring music was more than she could tolerate. In addition, she had also detected the characteristic sweetness of marijuana and noted the increasing uninhibitedness of some guests' behavior.

Deil was right; her dress was a bit too flirtatious for the boisterous crowd. At least Kelly assumed that's why she'd been getting more than her fair share of come-ons this evening. That plus the fact that she was unaccompanied. Barry had deserted her almost immediately following their arrival. She'd seen him cuddling with several beautiful young women since then.

Barry must have decided to use this party as a means of paying her back, Kelly decided. Her mind logically viewed his game plan. He'd heard about Deil's popularity with women and had been biding his time. Obviously, he saw tonight as his chance to get even.

Kelly sighed, sipped at her second glass of white wine, and silently berated herself for not forseeing something like this. But she'd been so intent on getting out and proving a point to Deil that she'd been oblivious to the possibility. Another sip of wine, another discreet check of the time. It was only eight; how could she go back to the apartment so early? What if Deil were entertaining Tara, or Cara, or whatever her name was?

Half an hour later Kelly had made up her mind to leave. She was out on the edge of the patio, vacillating over whether or not to wait for the cab she'd called, when a pair of lecherous arms grabbed her from behind. Kelly's reaction was instinctive and very painful for the unfortunate creep who'd been told by Barry that she was an easy lay. An infuriated Kelly stalked off, determined to find her own way home without waiting for a cab.

It was a rough trip home. Barry's house was nowhere

near Aspen's free shuttle service, not that she was too thrilled about the idea of waiting for a bus in the dark anyway. There were too many groups of young men wandering around. A number of them were bikers, cruising on their motorcycles, in town for a rally the following day. Then there was the little matter of her dress shoes, their slim heels completely unsuitable for walking. She made it home just after nine, her arrival in front of her apartment marked by the opening skyrocket of the fireworks display being staged on Aspen Mountain.

A swift glance up noted the colorful explosion before her eyes swung over to check her front bay window. It was dark. Good, that meant Deil must still be out with Tara. Kelly eagerly hurried up the stairs, put her key into the lock, and swung open the door. Her fingers momentarily groped in the darkness for the light switch before flicking it on and flooding the room with light.

Kelly's startled gasp mingled with Deil's exasperated sigh and a willowy redhead's moue of protest.

"You're home early," Deil noted.

But Kelly wasn't listening; she was consumed with jealousy at the sight of Deil sitting on her couch with a gorgeous woman clinging to him. All the standard primitive thoughts came to mind—clawing the other woman's eyes out, or breaking her arm, the one that was draped across Deil's shoulders. Kelly's eyes vented her resentment, glaring at Tara with such a look of unmitigated fury that the other woman took fright.

"I think I'd better go," Tara nervously suggested.

"But the fireworks are just starting," Deil protested.

"Yes, they are," Kelly agreed, her inflection unmistakably stating that there would soon be a set of matching fireworks inside this very apartment.

Another rocket went off, its echoing bang making Tara jump in fright.

"Kelly," Deil warned, his expression stern.

To her dismay, she felt the unmistakable prick of impending tears. What was wrong with her? There wasn't time to speculate; she had to get out of there before she made an idiot of herself. "I'm going to my room," she said with dignity.

In the safety of her own room she allowed the tears to fall, but choked back the sobs, for fear the sound might carry to the living room. There was no way she could justify her interest in Deil as being purely platonic, not in the face of this painful jealousy.

Kelly could hear the soft murmur of voices and then the sharp slam of the front door closing. Her shoulders sagged in defeat. So they'd left. Deil and Tara. Together. Probably went to Tara's place.

Well, what are you going to do? an inner voice demanded. *Sit in here crying your eyes out all night or go out there and watch the fireworks?* With a determined sniff, Kelly got up off her bed and headed down the hall toward the living room. Deil must have left without turning the lights off.

"You want to tell me what all that was about?" his voice quietly asked.

Kelly immediately stiffened and turned away from him. "What are you doing here?"

"I live here," Deil dryly retorted.

"I thought you left with Tara."

"Obviously not."

Kelly looked around as if expecting to find the redhead crouched behind the couch. "Where did she go?"

"Home."

"Why didn't you go with her?"

"She asked me not to. She lives only downstairs, just moved into Apartment 1A."

"I see."

Deil moved closer to catch a better look at Kelly's face. "Do you?"

She nodded.

"You've been crying," he softly accused.

Kelly saw no point in denying it, not with her obviously red-rimmed eyes. "This isn't going to work."

"What isn't?" He reached out to gently stroke her cheek. "Our living together or our dating other people?"

Kelly shifted uncomfortably, refusing to lie yet unwilling to reveal the depth of her emotions. "Both," she finally said.

With a shake of his head, Deil said, "I don't think so."

"No?" She took a step backward, dislodging his caressing hand.

"No," he repeated. "I think you've finally discovered what I've known for a while."

"What's that?"

"That it's useless to fight it."

"Fight what?"

Her pretended nonchalance made him smile. "You know what. This feeling between us."

"But that's just—"

"I know we've both tried to rationalize it," Deil interrupted. "But it's too strong."

"What are we going to do?"

"First off, you're going to stop sounding so scared."

"I'm not scared," she tried denying.

It didn't work. "Aren't you?" His look questioned her honesty.

"Well, what if I am? Wouldn't you be?"

"I am," Deil readily admitted.

"You are? Why?"

"Kelly, I want to be up front with you. No matter what there may be between us, I'm not ready for marriage. I really can't afford the responsibilities at this point in my career. So if you're looking for marriage . . ."

"I'm not."

"Are you sure?"

"I'm sure." She nodded.

Deil motioned her over to the couch and sat down beside her. "All right then, here's the game plan. I suggest we give ourselves a little time to see how a relationship might go between us."

Kelly looked at him in surprise. "You mean dating?"

Deil's expression was one of rueful self-mockery. "I guess that's what I mean."

"And what about our sleeping arrangements?" Kelly bluntly inquired.

"They remain the same."

"They do?"

"For the time being."

"How generous of you!" she sarcastically commended. "And what about Cara?

"Cara?" he repeated in confusion. "Oh, you mean Tara."

"And all the others," Kelly added.

"I assume you're inquiring about dating other people."

"Bull's-eye!"

"I don't want anyone else, Kelly. I want you." He ruined the romantic tenor of his reply by adding, "I started dating so much because I didn't plan on getting involved with you and I don't want to rush into anything."

"Don't put yourself out on my account!" Kelly flared, angered by his logical approach.

"I'm trying to be cautious."

"A case of if-you-can't-be-good-be-careful?" she snipped.

"Oh, but I can be good, my dear Watson. Very good. Shall I show you?"

Kelly nervously slid away from the silken promise of his voice "I was just . . ."

"Getting yourself in over your head, as usual," he inserted.

"I do not get in over my head," was her quick denial. Indignation added a bewitching sparkle to her eyes and an overall glow to her face.

"You look cute when you're angry," Deil took time out to say.

"So do you," she pertly retorted, disarmed by the coaxing appeal of his smile.

That smile turned into an all-out grin. "You know what? I really like you, Kelly Watson!"

"I'm glad," she grinned in return. "The feeling could well be mutual, English!"

He raised an inquiring eyebrow. "English?"

"If you can call me 'my dear Watson,' I can call you 'English.' Unless you'd prefer Holmes?"

Deil grimaced and shook his head.

Kelly tried again. "Sherlock?"

He tumbled her into his arms. "English will suffice. Or darling in a pinch."

"Darling," Kelly seductively murmured, her voice an expressive tool. But before Deil could act, she'd slipped off the couch. "Come look at the fireworks."

Taking him by the hand, she drew him over to the

floor-to-ceiling bay window. An imitation oriental rug fit into the three-sided alcove. Without a second thought Kelly gracefully sank down onto it, her fingers automatically stroking the rug's thick nap.

"What are you doing?" Deil indulgently inquired.

"Sitting down. Toss me a couple pillows from the couch, would you? Thanks." This as she deftly caught the flung cushion. "Come, join me."

Deil shrugged off his velvet jacket, tossing it over the back of the couch before loosening his tie and joining her on the floor. As he watched she stretched out on her stomach, resting her elbows on the rug and her chin on the heels of her palms. "I love fireworks," she murmured, watching another shower of red, white, and blue fire rain down from the sky.

"I gathered that much," was his mocking reply.

"You can see them better from this angle," she said somewhat defensively.

"I was referring to the temper tantrum you threw when you walked in on Tara and me."

"Oh, those fireworks."

"Mmm," he nodded. "It appears that there are all kinds, hmm?"

Kelly ignored the inflection at the end of his comment, concentrating instead on the grand finale, a continuous stream of flashing, screaming, booming, fireworks. Nonstop explosions lit the entire sky with their chromatic display. The windows had been opened during the heat of the day, and now the reverberating echoes floated through the screens. All too soon, the pyrotechnics stopped.

"It's over." There was a tinge of childish disappointment in her voice.

"No, it's not," Deil denied.

"Yes, it is," Kelly maintained. "They've set off all the fireworks."

"I wasn't talking about the display on Aspen Mountain. I was talking about the display lying here beside me. You, my dear Watson!"

"You wouldn't be trying to flirt with me now, would you, English?"

"I can't answer that on the grounds that it may incriminate me!"

"I suppose you picked up that phrase from your father, the international lawyer?"

Deil rolled onto his side, the movement bringing him closer. "You'd be amazed at how many things I've picked up along the way," he softly murmured, sparks of lambent passion flaring in his hazel eyes.

Kelly found herself rolling toward him, responding to the beckoning warmth of his gaze. Deil lifted a hand to feather across her face, teasing her lashes, tracing her nose, tantalizing her mouth. Kelly's lips parted, her tongue flicking out to taste his skin. She was amazed to feel him shudder at the tiny caress.

Encouraged by the success of her first effort, she reached out to touch his face as he'd touched hers. Her surveying fingers found his lashes to be extravagantly long and surprisingly soft, his nose straight and undaunted, and his lips waiting for her touch. Kelly's tongue still lightly circled the tip of his index finger, which she'd flirtatiously trapped between her teeth. Deil's caressing turnabout was to ensnare her surveying finger, his tongue evocatively painting its trembling length before darting to the ultrasensitive web between her fingers.

Kelly felt like someone had lit a sparkler inside of her, the showering embers searing the remnants of her patience. Able to wait no longer, she slid her hand from his mouth and guided his lips to hers. Meanwhile her lips parted to release his hand, which then combed through her hair, gripping her in a sure hold.

Their kiss held no signs of tentativeness or uncertainty. It was an explosion of melding mouths and cavorting tongues. Kelly moaned and rolled closer, her nylon-clad legs brushing against the rough denim of his jeans. Her hand slid to his nape, sensuously kneading the sinewy muscles before slipping her fingers beneath the still buttoned collar of his shirt.

Deil had a far easier time of it than she did. The neckline of her dress was barely held together by three loosely tied bows. A gentle tug on the dangling end of each one loosened the material to reveal a full slip the same honey color as her lightly tanned skin.

Their kisses wandered, as did their hands. Deil kissed the line of her throat; Kelly undid his burgundy silk tie. He mouthed the tip of a now bare shoulder; she unbuttoned the top three buttons of his shirt. At the touch of his warm mouth on the softness of her breast, fireworks of another kind flashed behind her closed eyelids, blinding her with their brilliance. One hand ran through the unruly waves of his hair, pressing him closer, while her other hand undid the remaining buttons of his shirt, massaging its way from his lean waist to his powerful shoulders.

She liked the way Deil murmured his pleasure and found her own responses becoming more vocal. The excitement, the tautening anticipation was so intense that it had to be verbalized, yet no words had been devised to describe the feelings coursing through her. So instead, Kelly settled for half-muffled, expressive sighs that eloquently communicated the measure of her pleasure. The result was a sensual plainsong that Deil likened to a purr, and responded to by petting her all the more!

When Kelly's sinuously pliant form arched closer, her legs entangled with his, her hips seeking the surging power of his. Deil knew he had to be the one to call a halt. Now before it was too late!

He eased away from her restraining hands, rolling with pantherlike grace to his feet. In the silence of the room Kelly could hear the heavy unsteadiness of his breathing, sense the tremors of self-control he was imposing on his fully aroused body.

"Why did you start this if you didn't mean to finish it?" was her dazed demand. Kelly's brain immediately scrambled to regain control of her wayward tongue.

"Because the fireworks were getting out of hand, and I didn't want either one of us getting burned in the explosion." We're going to go slow and easy if it kills me! Deil added silently. *And at this rate it just might!*

CHAPTER SIX

Kelly woke up the next morning in a deliciously euphoric frame of mind. She'd dreamed about Deil all night, racy dreams that made her blood boil. They were going to spend the day together and the prospect made her throw off the covers and jump out of bed. Her nightgown was replaced with a clean bra and matching panties.

Standing before her closet, Kelly tried to choose an appropriate outfit. It didn't take her long to go through everything hanging in the closet. Clothes had never been a high priority item with her before. Extra money had always gone toward her art, buying new tools or replenishing supplies.

Now she wished she'd splurged a few more times. "Oh, well," she teased herself with a philosophical shrug. "At least my figure is good. Except for . . ." Kelly absentmindedly reached down to rub the small scar at the back of her knee.

Perhaps the time was right to tell Deil about everything . . . the accident . . . David. *If you don't get dressed soon,* she silently delivered a scolding, *there won't be time to do anything!* Her freshly laundered stretch denim jeans were swiftly pulled on and fastened. A T-shirt was then tugged on over her head. The white cotton front was colorfully adorned with the representation of mountain peaks and a lake of steaming coffee while the words THE LEFT BANK were printed on the back. It was one of several tops custom designed for the café where Kelly worked a few evenings a week. While the pay wasn't exceptional, the tips were good and the café was the source of her free supply of day old croissants, not to mention T-shirts!

Her dark hair didn't require much attention, which was why Kelly liked the short style. A few strokes with a brush and she was ready to face the world. Too much makeup would have clashed with her casual appearance, so she kept it simple—eye liner and lip gloss.

She followed a delicious smell to their kitchen, where she found Deil fixing breakfast. "Mmm, what smells so good?"

"Me?" Deil modestly suggested.

"Not unless you're using maple-scented aftershave."

"Then it must be the pancakes. They're all ready. If you'd care to take a seat, my dear Watson."

"Sure thing, English," she jauntily retorted.

Deil served the pancakes with a rueful shake of his head. "I think I may regret allowing you to call me that."

"I could always go back to Sherlock," she offered with overwhelming helpfulness.

"No, you couldn't."

Kelly waited until he'd joined her at the undersized kitchen table before asking, "What would you like to do today?"

Deil looked up from his pancake-covered plate, his eyes consuming her instead of his breakfast. Silently his gaze told her what he'd like to do—to her—and Kelly found the experience unbelievably potent.

Syrup dripped unnoticed from her half-raised fork as it

hovered in mid-air. Not a word had been spoken, but the message had been transmitted with evocative clarity. His eyes touched on her face and body like tangible caresses, his intent hypnotically clear. The eloquence of such visual communication transcended the world of words, making them seem ineffective in comparison.

"We'd better wait, though," Deil huskily whispered.

Kelly didn't need to ask, Wait for what? She knew, they both knew, that one day soon they'd make love, passionately and unreservedly. This period of waiting just made the anticipation all the keener!

"How about a trip to Ashcroft?" If Deil noticed that her voice was breathier than normal, he made no comment.

"One of the local ghost towns?"

"How'd you know? Have you been there already?"

"No, I haven't done much sight-seeing."

"Too busy painting the town?" she suggested with a small measure of jealousy.

"I'm a writer, not a painter. The whole thing was an exercise in futility anyway."

"What was?"

"Dating other women," he replied, taking a sip of coffee before elaborating. "No matter how many I went out with, I still had to come back to you, here in this apartment, with just the two of us."

Along with the ghost of roommates past, Kelly thought to herself, remembering Deil's comment the first day he'd arrived. Never one to skirt around an issue, Kelly said, "I seem to recall your assuring me that you had no intention of getting seriously involved with anyone at this stage of your life."

"That's right," he cautiously agreed.

"I'd really like to know what's made you so gun-shy."

95

Deil searched her face, as if looking for some sign to indicate this was the time to tell Kelly about it. Finding what he was looking for, he began. "Well, Fiona was incredibly possessive. She refused to believe my feelings for her did not justify marriage although I tried again and again to make that clear. By the time I convinced her that I meant what I said, the damage had been done."

"And you've judged all other women by her standards ever since?"

"Not all other women."

"But I have the dubious honor of restoring your faith in womankind?"

Deil had to laugh at Kelly's less than enthusiastic expression. "You, my dear Watson, have the uncanny ability of making me laugh, even if it's at myself."

"I'm glad you realize how funny you can be, English."

"I wonder if you realize how sexy you can be? It isn't going to be easy, you know."

"What isn't?"

"Not taking you to bed!"

The drive to Ashcroft was a ruggedly scenic one down Castle Creek Valley, the valley neighboring Maroon Bells. Here the landscape seemed more softly alpine, the vegetation more verdant. Horses grazed in meadows of wildflowers, immune to the beauty they were cheerfully chomping.

Kelly and Deil strolled along Ashcroft's wooden boardwalk, hands clasped, fingers entwined. They stopped to look at each of the buildings, some of which had recently been restored. The abandoned log cabins seemed small and dark when compared to the grand spaciousness of the surrounding landscape.

There was a "resident ghost," a volunteer from the

Aspen Historical Society, on duty in the Blue Mirror Saloon. The wooden walls exhibited photographs of Ashcroft in more affluent times. Deil pointed out one in particular, taken of a bustling main street on the Fourth of July 1882.

"Eerie to think that was only a hundred years ago," he murmured.

"Goes to show you how much can happen in a hundred years," Kelly returned.

"Especially in this country." Deil's face wore a look of disapproval that was echoed in his tone. "In Europe the buildings have stood for many hundreds of years, not just one. Yet here in the States so much of our heritage is allowed to disintegrate, that is if it isn't demolished first."

"I think Americans are beginning to realize the importance of maintaining our historical landmarks," Kelly defended her countrymen. "Ashcroft is an example; it's been renovated."

"But a majority of its funds still depend on donations." Deil indicated the box for that purpose located near the door and dropped some money in it before taking Kelly's arm and going back outside.

"I will say one thing—those photographs didn't look quite the way Hollywood portrays the old West, did they." Her expression turned the question into a statement of fact.

"John Wayne would've had to bend over in half to get through the front door. And I've seen tents bigger than some of these cabins."

They walked on down the boardwalk to the hotel at the end of town. "I haven't been in this building since they finished working on it."

Deil doffed an imaginary Stetson and dusted it with his

elbow. He then squinted his hazel eyes à la Clint Eastwood and drawled, "After you, ma'am," before ushering her inside.

Kelly joined in the play-acting, lifting the hem of a long make-believe dress.

"We'd like a room with a view," Deil loftily informed a bare two-by-four. "Upstairs? Fine."

Again he helped her up the stairs to the second floor. It was indeed a room with a view, a view and little else!

"Not much privacy," Kelly lamented.

"Why, what did you have in mind, ma'am?" Deil drawled, his expression as rascally roguish as any she'd seen in a Western.

"I imagine it gets mighty lonely out here for a cowboy," she mused, flirtatiously hiking up her fictitious dress.

"Mighty lonely," Deil agreed, tossing the nonexistent Stetson out the open window. One arm swept her into a tight embrace. "*Yore* the *purtiest* thing west of the Mississippi!" The compliment was growled against her ear as he nuzzled the sensitive hollows.

Kelly slid her arms around his neck, tugging on the strands of hair that grew low on the nape. Deil's lips slid along the line of her jaw before settling on her mouth for a kiss as immodestly lascivious as any she'd read about in a Western historical romance.

"There's something to be said for the twentieth century," Deil muttered, his fingers tracing the mountainous outlines printed on her T-shirt. "You'd never have gotten away with wearing something like this in 1882."

"You approve of my T-shirt?"

"I approve of what's beneath it. You've given an entirely new dimension to the idea of mountain climbing!" Her three-dimensional, sensual topography held his unwavering attention.

Kelly's bemused eyes flickered down to her shirtfront and saw that the T-shirt's printed mountain peaks happened to coincide with her own blossoming breasts. Then his lips lowered to tease hers and she was lost once more to his sensual expertise.

Deil's arms must have been unusually long, for they were able to wrap around her and still leave his hands free to investigate her curvaceousness. He began slowly circling the underside of each breast, skillfully ascending the fullness, working his way up from base to sensitive apex. Once there, the tips of his lean fingers skimmed the surging peaks, cajoling them both to taut attention. All his evocative explorations were done on top of her T-shirt, the seductive fondling leaving her knees weak. Consequently, she depended even more upon Deil for her support, her pliant body leaning heavily into his.

The sound of footsteps beneath them reluctantly and abruptly brought their embrace to an end. "Just as well there are no beds up here," was Deil's muttered decision. "As it is I may well have to go take a dip in the river."

"But the water's ice cold!"

"That's the idea," he mockingly acknowledged.

Instead of taking a dip in the river, they ate lunch at an out-of-the-way cookhouse. Reenergized by the day's specialty, Hungarian goulash, they decided to take a walk. They stopped to rest on a bench picturesquely located near the rushing river.

"You never told me what happened at Barry's party," Deil reminded her. "Why did you leave early?"

"It wasn't my cup of tea." *Which is probably the biggest understatement I've ever made.*

"Is Barry your cup of tea?"

"Nope," she answered with a vehement shake of her head. "The charming prince suddenly reverted back to a frog!" Kelly was unaware of the bitter anger coloring her voice as the shoddiness of Barry's behavior came to mind.

"Did something happen that I should know about?" Deil's scowl threatened dire consequences for Barry were she to answer affirmatively.

"Suffice it to say that we will no longer be seeing each other."

"I'm glad you've finally decided to dump Luce."

"Oh? Why's that?"

"The same reason you had for scaring off my date last night!"

"There's something I'd like to talk to you about," she admitted somewhat hesitantly.

"Go ahead," Deil invited, thinking she meant to own up to her jealousy.

Kelly surprised him by saying, "It's about that night you came to my room to cover me up."

"You want to talk about David?" he correctly surmised, not looking very thrilled at the prospect.

"You talked about Fiona."

He couldn't fault her argument. "I'm listening."

"David Pitman and I were going together a year and a half ago. We'd known each other for several months and I thought it was love. David was an avid skier. He taught me how to ski and we spent a lot of our time on the slopes. Then, well . . ." Her narrative was faltering. "There was an accident," she baldly stated. "To this day, I can't say exactly what happened. One minute I was gliding down the mountain, free as a bird, and the next I was laying in

100

a crumpled heap. The ski patrol rushed me to the hospital where they had to operate."

"The scar on the back of your knee," Deil remembered.

Kelly nodded. "They removed the cartilage. The damage was so extensive that at first the doctors feared I'd always walk with a limp. That's when David took off. He couldn't cope with 'physical imperfections,' " she bitterly quoted.

"Hey," he softly murmured. "I'm sorry."

"I really haven't thought about it for some time, but your asking about the scar sort of brought it all back."

Deil shook his head in disgust, recalling his high-handed behavior. "You should've slugged me!"

"There have been times when I've been tempted, believe me!"

"When I rearranged the kitchen cabinets?" he guessed, the beginnings of a grin tugging his mobile mouth.

"That was one of the times, yes."

"How about when I attempted to commit harakiri on your intimate apparel?" Now he wore a decided grin, and his eyes reflected a devilish twinkle.

"That was another one," she admitted.

"Perhaps I was trying to sabotage all your bras so you'd be forced into going without one!" was his devious suggestion.

"I hadn't thought of that."

"Neither had I, actually, but the idea does have its high points!" His caressive sideways glance focused on her shirtfront.

"I may never wear this T-shirt again," Kelly muttered half under her breath before changing the subject. "Listen, I wanted to ask you if you'd be interested in going to see ABT II perform up at Snowmass?"

"American Ballet Theatre?"

"The secondary company, yes."

"I'd be delighted."

"I got a pair of tickets in exchange for a small panel I exhibited at the art fair."

"Bartering again, hmm?"

Kelly grinned. "Just don't let the IRS in on it," she pleaded. "Knowing how they work, I'd probably be taxed on those two tickets!"

"Your secret's safe with me, ma'am." He'd really gotten the cowboy accent down pat. "I'll protect you from those varmints!"

While it would have been nice to linger there, they had to hurry home because there was a Sherlock Holmes movie on television early that evening that they wanted to see.

"I love Basil Rathbone in this role," Kelly said through a mouthful of popcorn, happily rocking in her wicker chair.

"Holmes never actually said, 'Elementary, my dear Watson.' It was invented by Hollywood, you know."

"Another myth bites the dust!" Kelly dramatically sighed.

"Here, drown your sorrows in this." He handed her the bowl of popcorn.

"Thanks." Kelly grabbed another handful of the buttery snack before taking a sip of root beer.

Deil shook his head in amused disbelief. "It seems sacrilegious to be drinking root beer out of a brandy glass."

"Look on it as a widening of your horizons, English!" She stuck another handful of popcorn into her mouth before exclaiming, "Hey, is this the movie with the Creeper in it?"

"The Creeper? Sounds like a fugitive from a B horror movie!"

"No, he's the bad guy . . ."

"The antagonist," Deil literarily identified.

Kelly nodded. "He does a lot of that too. Anyway, he's the one who's strangling everyone."

"Thank you very much for giving away the ending."

"But was that the real ending, or was I only using that as a red herring to throw you off the track of the real villain?"

Deil eyed her suspicously. "Did the Creeper do it?"

"You'll have to wait and see!"

The Thursday night performance of the ballet happened to coincide with the arrival of Deil's first installment of his advance from his English publisher. To celebrate the event, Kelly invited her illustrious writer of a roommate out to dinner, her treat. They had the usual fight beforehand.

"You've already supplied the ballet tickets. I'll supply the dinner."

"The ballet tickets were given to me," she pointed out.

"In exchange for a piece of your work."

"Haven't you ever had a woman offer to pay for your dinner before? Is that it?"

"You make me sound like a kept man," Deil complained.

"If you're kept, that must mean I'm the keeper!"

"You like the sound of that, don't you, my dear Watson."

"I must confess it holds a certain appeal to the possessive side of my nature," she archly returned.

"I didn't know you had any other part to your nature," he mocked.

"Cheap shot!" she cried, throwing a pillow at him.

Deil, who by now was accustomed to her off-center aim, dodged to the right and missed getting hit. "You'll never pitch for the Yankees," he informed her.

"If you won't let me take you out for dinner, then I'll just cook something for you here," she warned.

"That's blackmail!" he protested with a deliberately appalled expression.

"That's right," she agreed. "I know how much you enjoyed those special pork chops I made. You remember, the ones with the rice breakfast cereal coating."

Deil grimaced in distaste. "Snap, crackle, and oink."

"So you said at the time," she grinned.

"Okay!" He threw up his hands in mocking surrender. "You may take me to dinner, anything, so long as I never have to see those pork chops again!"

Kelly had the perfect dress for their evening out. It was one she'd gotten on sale from one of Aspen's many clothing boutiques. Kelly had fallen in love with the deceptively simple little number in varying shades of green silk at first sight. Now as she stood before the full-length mirror on the back of her bedroom door, she was very pleased with her appearance. Very pleased, indeed!

Her shoes, all straps and slender heels, added a good three inches to her height. A pair of elegant silklike panty hose covered her shapely legs. Her makeup was concentrated on her eyes, for Kelly privately considered them to be one of her best features. She'd brushed glimmering emerald shadow on the lids, adding a touch of a lighter shade at the edges to widen her eyes. Eye liner and mascara had both been carefully applied to accentuate the slant of what her brothers had teasingly called her "cat's eyes." Tonight the almond-shaped orbs did indeed resemble a playful feline's, right down to the mischievous sparkle.

Deil eyed her in silent appreciation, which gave Kelly time to admire the handsome picture he made in a suit and tie. Could this be the same wrinkled suit he'd arrived in? Its cut was immaculate, the smooth tailoring showing off his fine physique. A comb had been used in an effort to contain the unruly waves of his hair, his "bangs" almost brushing the matching darkness of his eyebrows. Hazel eyes gazed into hers, his ravishing look telegraphing a passionate message.

"Words fail me." His voice was husky. "You look . . ."

"All right?"

"Definitely all right," he confirmed, in that same husky tone.

"Good?"

"Better than good."

"Gorgeous, ravishing, fantabulous?" she teasingly suggested.

"You're all of the above."

"So are you."

"Why thank you, roomie!"

Kelly came closer to mockingly punch his arm. Her closeness made her realize that the added inches of her heels had made them the same height.

Deil, noting the same thing, murmured, "For once we see eye to eye!"

"Enjoy it while you can," she impudently suggested.

"Oh, I intend to," was Deil's velvety assurance. He leaned closer, her added inches saving him from lowering his head. When his lips just brushed hers, he added, "After dinner! Shall we be off?" Stepping back, he offered her his arm with courtly courtesy.

"By all means."

The performance was being given up at Snowmass as part of a month's worth of dance activities. The ballet was lovely, and the artist in Kelly responded to the dancer's lyrical movements. Afterward, they drove back to Aspen for a late supper. Kelly was amazed to discover that Deil knew the owner of the small restaurant she'd selected.

"I thought you didn't know anyone from Aspen," she hissed as the beaming owner led them to his best table.

"I don't," Deil returned, his humor evident by the right-sided tug of his smile. "George is from New York!"

The restaurant, one of several in restored Victorian mansions, was decorated with a flower motif—the rose— in deference to its name. Selected works of art with the rose as subject matter were tastefully hung around the paneled walls. An antique cherrywood bar shone from numerous polishings over the years.

"Like it?" Deil asked, holding out a chair for her.

Kelly quickly sank into the plushly upholstered seat before responding. "It's lovely."

"Thanks." George Denton smiled. "We tried to retain as much of the original atmosphere as possible." He left them with a pair of hand-printed menus so they could make their selection.

"I've never been here before," she leaned across the table to tell Deil.

"That surprises me."

Kelly defended her omission. "There are over one hundred places to have dinner or lunch in Aspen. We've got pubs, cafeterias, bars, bistros, even subterranean dives, as well as several internationally known restaurants."

"I believe the latter group is the one George is hoping to join. That or the subterranean dives—I can't be certain which. But you omitted to mention cafés in your dining list."

"You would bring up work."

"I just wanted to say that The Left Bank has the best help in town, let alone the best T-shirts!"

"You're prejudiced," she accused.

"Because you work there?"

"No, because they get the London *Times* for you to read."

"I'll have you know, my dear Watson, that it is referred to as *theee Times*." He deliberately drew out the long vowel, his English accent unmistakable.

"Oh, I get it," Kelly said sotto voce, her accent just as deliberately American. "A case of the royal *thee*, huh?"

"Are we going to exchange puns or order dinner?"

"Dinner," she immediately selected. "If I'm given a choice, food always wins out."

"I'll have to remember that," Deil murmured, his low pitch unmistakably intimate.

The arrival of the waiter prevented his further elaboration. Kelly chose the chicken breast in lemon butter, Deil the fresh trout.

While they waited for their meal, Kelly related some of Aspen's colorful past. "The city was founded by prospectors who suspected that these mountains were full of precious metals. They were right, at least as far as silver was concerned. The largest silver nugget in the world came from the Smuggler Mine near here."

"I'm impressed!"

"If you'd like to learn more, you should pay a visit to Stallard House. That's the Aspen Historical Society's museum house."

"I'll keep that in mind," he promised. "But right now I'd like to know how you know so much about Aspen. You should work for their tourist bureau."

"I already do," she calmly informed him. "When things get hectic during the winter season."

"You're always surprising me, do you know that?"

There was a momentary pause in the conversation as their food was served. Noting Kelly's slight grimace a few minutes later, Deil asked, "What's wrong? Is the lemon butter too tart?"

"No, it's delicious. It's just . . . ."

"What?" he prompted.

"Your fish."

His face was blank. "My what?"

"Your fish. Trout," she corrected. "It's staring at me."

Deil picked up a garnish of parsley and covered the fish's head. "There. Is that better?"

"Yes, thanks."

Exchanging light banter with Deil made the time fly, and they were one of the restaurant's last customers. Their bill was tactfully placed midway between the two of them, on the table's neutral zone.

"My treat," Kelly reminded him as Deil automatically reached for his wallet.

"Sure?"

"Of course I'm sure." She swung her small shoulder bag from its resting position at the back of her chair. Comb, lipstick, used tickets . . . no wallet! Dismayed, Kelly looked again, carefully going through the pitifully few

108

items in the purse. Where could her wallet have gone? Had someone stolen it? If so, when? Marshaling her chaotic thoughts, it suddenly came to her that she'd changed purses for tonight. Her wallet, she could picture it so clearly now, was sitting on top of her dresser, back at the apartment!

"Something wrong?" Deil inquired.

"Wrong?" she stalled, trying to come up with a graceful way out of this.

"Having trouble finding your wallet?" he guessed.

"Quite a lot, actually. I left it at home."

"At home?"

"Afraid so."

"Some fine date you turn out to be!" he teased. "Invite me out and then stick me with the bill."

"I am not sticking you with the bill!" she vehemently denied. "I'll charge it!"

"You will?"

"Certainly."

"Don't you keep your charge cards in your wallet?" he inquired with dry humor.

"Oh."

"By that I take it I'm paying the bill?"

Kelly nodded, restrained by the waiter's reappearance.

"It's all your fault, anyway!" she accused Deil as soon as the waiter was out of earshot.

"My fault!" he repeated in astonishment. "How do you figure that?"

"You wished it on me."

"My dear Watson, if my wishes came true, we'd both be in bed right now!" he wryly retorted.

"Oh? Tired, are you?" she saucily inquired.

"What I was envisioning had nothing to do with sleep and everything to do with—"

"I know what it has to do with," she censored.

Deil's look was a caress. "Then someday soon, we'll have to do it!"

CHAPTER SEVEN

"You're next!" A blue-jeaned young man yelled out the warning to Deil and Kelly. They were standing at the base of the Aspen Highlands ski lift, more commonly known as the Sky Ride. The two-seater chairs were automatically swinging around the bottom tower, immediately ready to pick up new passengers for the return trip up.

They'd chosen a beautiful day for their excursion, sunny though quite warm. Taking their specified places, they stood waiting for the next chair to scoop them up. It did so with the customary swing afterward. Kelly gripped Deil's arm in fear, a wave of panic washing over her.

"Hey, are you all right?" Deil asked in concern after lowering the safety bar in front of them.

"I'm fine," Kelly murmured, shaking off the shrouds of alarm. "Just getting my air legs!"

"And a nice pair of legs they are too!"

"Why, thank you."

"Think nothing of it."

They faced the mountain on their ascent, skimming high above the treetops and landing high above the tree line! The panoramic view from the top presented a jumbled sea of rugged mountains. It also presented a mass of dark clouds rapidly approaching from the west. Soon the booming peals of thunder could be heard to the accompaniment of flickering forks of lightning.

Kelly and Deil joined the other visitors in a rush for cover. The steep roof of a supply shed provided some measure of protection from lashing hailstones and drenching sheets of rain. They huddled for shelter as best they could. Summer thunderstorms tended to be intense in nature and brief in duration. This one was no exception.

"Awesome, isn't it?" Deil lowered his head to speak into Kelly's ear, his lips brushing the damp tendrils of hair that were plastered to her cheek.

Another fierce gust splattered them with rain, dampening their unprotected jeans. Kelly shivered and gathered her Windbreaker closer around her.

Feeling her tremor, he asked, "Not scared, are you?"

"No, I just got some water down my back. That rain is coooold!"

"Poor baby!" he commiserated. "Maybe I can warm you up." His hands drew her closer and unzipped her jacket.

"What are you doing?" she protested. "I'm already cold."

"Trust me."

There was no mistaking the sportive humor in her tone. "Where have I heard that one before?"

He unzipped his own jacket and pulled her in snuggly against his chest. "Better?"

Kelly nodded, then teasingly poked him in the ribs.

Deil flinched away, letting a stream of cold air in between them. "Don't do that!" he scolded. "I'm ticklish."

"Where?" She poked him again. "There?"

"Right there," he confirmed, grabbing her fingers.

"Any more of that and I might go tumbling right off this mountain."

Kelly's shiver turned into a distinct shudder at the thought of Deil falling, at the fear of falling itself. Deil mistakenly attributed her tremor to a particularly close clap of thunder. His hands reached under her jacket to soothe her back, slipping under the edge of her T-shirt.

"Oooh!" Kelly inhaled a startled gasp.

"What's wrong?"

"Your hand's cold."

"Sorry." He offered the apology with a boyish grin.

"Maybe I should warm it up," she provocatively suggested.

"And how do you propose to do that?" Deil lowered his hands to ask in his reporter's monotone.

"This isn't a press conference at the House of Commons, you know," she reprimanded. "You're supposed to sound wildly romantic."

"On top of a mountain, when I'm freezing?"

"I thought macho males were supposed to be invincible."

"And real men don't eat quiche, I suppose?"

"You read that, too, hmm? No; scratch that. What a silly question to ask a compulsive reader."

"I am not compulsive."

"No? You're the only person I know who reads the nation's temperatures!"

"Slander! Slander!" he cried.

"So sue me," she grinned.

"Why bother when I've got more immediate ways of punishing you?" He lifted his cold hands, placing both of them on the small of her back before trailing them up her spine.

"Cad!"

"I've never been called a cad before."

"How does it feel?" Kelly borrowed his reporter's inflection.

"I'm not sure."

"How does this feel?" She placed her unprotected hands on his back.

"Cold," he acknowledged in a conversational tone of voice.

"Hey, look! The rain's stopped."

"Just in time. Come on, let's get back down to warmer climes before I freeze my—"

Kelly quickly covered his mouth with her hand. "You weren't going to say anything naughty, were you?"

Deil shook his head like a schoolboy being reprimanded by a teacher.

"Good," she approved.

"You're good," he murmured, roguishly curling his tongue into the heart of her palm.

"So are you!" She returned the compliment with a saucy wink.

Arm in arm they made their way over the hail-covered ground back to the departure point. Kelly experienced the same rush of panic once they were off the ground and seated in the swinging chair lift. Once they were on their way, the buffeting winds rocked them to and fro. Whereas coming up they had been facing the mountain, now there was nothing but a huge expanse of space in front of them. Kelly felt herself hurtling, hurtling back in time to her skiing accident, when she'd fallen forward into nothingness and excruciating pain.

Panic rose from deep within her, causing her to shrink back in alarm. Her abrupt movement made the chair sway all the more. *Stay calm,* she silently ordered herself in an attempt to restore order to her churning emotions. The order might have been successful had the chair lift not precipitately halted. The unexpected cessation of their descent was the straw that broke the back of her control. Kelly gripped Deil's arm with a fear-crazed strength that made him wince.

"It's all right," he assured her, covering her hand with his. "They must've stopped the lift until this wind calms down a little. Should only be a few minutes. Nice view from up here, isn't it?"

When Kelly made no response, he turned to look at her more closely. Her face didn't reflect momentary uneasiness, but blind fear!

"Kelly, come here," he softly requested, easing her closer and wrapping a protective arm around her. He guided her head to rest on his shoulder and shut her eyes with gentle kisses. "Are you afraid of heights?"

"I don't know." Her words were muffled by the collar of his jacket, and Deil had to lower his head to catch them before the wind whipped them away.

"Is it the height that's bothering you?"

"It felt like I was falling," she shuddered.

He gathered her closer, or at least as close as he safely could under the circumstances. "Here, hold on to me. You can't go anywhere if I've got you. It's okay. You're not going anywhere; you're not going to fall." Deil crooned the reassurances over and over.

"It was the accident," she choked. "I haven't been on a ski lift since then."

"Damn!" Deil softly cursed himself. "I should've known you'd be upset after what you told me."

"There was no way you could have foreseen this. I

didn't even think of it." The mere mention of the accident had increased the waves of her panic. "Talk to me," she pleaded, trying to keep her head above the turbulent swell.

Recognizing her cry for help, Deil began talking in a deep, reassuring tone about nothing in particular and privately worrying how long they would be stuck dangling above the mountain.

Finally the chair began to slowly move again, resuming its downward descent. Kelly found it more harrowing to be moving in the dark, so she unburrowed her face from Deil's shoulder and opened her eyes. By looking backward she was able to avoid thinking about all the empty space before them. They arrived at one of the lift's two changing points a short time later. While thankful that the ride wasn't all in one go, Kelly worried about mustering up the courage to manage the next two sections.

Suspecting her reservations, Deil suggested stopping at the panoramic restaurant for a lunch break. Kelly refused the offer of food, but accepted a cup of strong coffee. Seated well away from the open view, they talked about her anxiety attack.

"It's stupid to be afraid of heights when I live eight thousand feet up," she maintained in disgust.

"What's stupid about it?"

"Deil, I live in the heart of the Rockies."

"I had noticed," he commented wryly with a glance out the window.

"I love the mountains. How can I be afraid of them?"

"It's not the mountains you're afraid of," he clarified. "It's the fear of falling."

"Which doesn't excuse it."

"Why should you need an excuse? You're human, aren't you?"

"Of course I am, but that's no . . ."

". . . excuse. Yes, I know." Deil shook his head at her. "Are you embarrassed that you showed me a sign of vulnerability?"

"Vulnerability is a polite way of putting it. I made an idiot of myself."

"In whose eyes? Certainly not mine."

"You're just trying to be nice," she dismissed.

"Hey, this is me, your roommate, remember? The hard-hitting political analyst and soon-to-be famous author who always tells the truth."

"Always?"

"Well," he drawled in recollection. "There was one occasion when I said Sally hadn't painted our father's car with shaving cream when I knew she had." His confession worked, bringing a hoped-for smile to Kelly's lips.

"I think I might have done the right thing in letting you stay at my apartment, English," she huskily murmured, genuine appreciation reflected in her green eyes.

"My dear Watson, was there any doubt?"

"There speaks the voice of modesty."

"One of my many attributes," he acknowledged with a polish of his knuckles.

His teasing banter helped keep the fear at bay, but the moment to continue their downward descent couldn't be put off indefinitely. Deil kept a firm possession of her hand and a comforting arm around her shoulders as they walked to the departure station for the next chair lift. With a minimum of fuss they were off, once more riding above the treetops.

Kelly felt warmed by Deil's constant attention, his watchful scanning of her features. "Want a Hershey bar?"

he asked after one particularly tricky point, the bumpy overpass of a metal support tower.

Kelly looked at the proffered chocolate wrapper. "It's Nestlé's."

"So it is."

"My mother warned me about strange men offering me candy," she tried joking, then took the chocolate, grateful for the distraction.

Although the remainder of the trip was uneventful, Kelly was still relieved to get to the bottom all in one piece.

"You managed that beautifully!" Deil congratulated her, dropping a proud kiss on her forehead. "How's it feel to be back on terra firma?"

"Great. I think I'll stick to safe things like picnics from now on!"

It was several days before they had the time to go on another excursion. Kelly had two commissioned panels to complete for a redecorated $250,000 condominium and Deil had ten more chapters to revise for his publisher.

Whenever Kelly worked evenings at The Left Bank, Deil had taken to showing up a short while before she was scheduled to leave and then taking her home. It was this very subject they were discussing as Deil drove east on Highway 82 toward Independence Pass.

"I still say it's theee *Times* that you're coming to see, not me," Kelly maintained.

"I've survived without seeing theee *Times,*" Deil defended himself, skillfully veering around a bicyclist puffing at the steep uphill grade.

"Only by making do with *The New York Times.*"

"I have to keep on top of things."

"Really?" she seductively purred, reaching out to evocatively stroke his thigh.

"Stop that!" He kiddingly slapped her hand away. "Any more of that and we'll go right over the edge, and I'm not referring only to this mountain! I read the newspaper every day to keep on top of developing political situations across the world."

"Very noble of you. I never knew political news was reported on the sports page."

"I like baseball," he had to admit.

"So I noticed." She'd caught him watching the games on TV.

"That's one of the things I miss in England. Baseball."

"And orange juice," she added, remembering his first night in her apartment.

"I wasn't wearing my contacts that night," Deil explained, also remembering that night. "That's why I bumped into the furniture."

"Sure it is," she magnanimously excused him, laughing at the fist he mockingly threatened her with. She was tempted to catch his hand in hers, but she knew that this stretch of road demanded both hands on the wheel. "What else did you miss in England?"

"Round doorknobs, soft toilet paper . . ."

"Wait a minute. Round doorknobs?"

"Mmm. Most European doors have handles instead of knobs."

"I didn't know that," she said before instructing him to turn right into the next campground.

"Campground?" he repeated. "I thought we were just going for a picnic. What kind of guy do you take me for?"

"A nice guy who's going to turn right into the next campground," was her prompt response.

"Nice?" Deil complained, flipping the Chevette's turn signal.

"How about a devious, intelligent, handsome devil?"

"That's better," he approved with a grin.

They left the car at the campground and walked the rest of the way. Deil had the rucksack full of food on his back, while Kelly carried nothing at all. Upset by this uneven distribution of the supplies, he handed her the plaid blanket. They walked by several possible sites before coming upon the perfect one. Rimmed by pines and quivering aspens, it afforded a lovely view of the surrounding mountains and rapid river.

Deil watched in amusement as Kelly unwrapped the food with evident anticipation. "I meant to tell you I replaced that cold chicken with black cherry yogurt," he absently noted.

"If you did, I'll throw you in the river!" she threatened.

"After you!" He lunged at her.

"Behave," she attempted to order sternly, but a threatening grin weakened the affect. "Here's the chicken, macaroni salad, fresh rolls, baby tomatoes . . ."

"My dear Watson, those are known as to-mah-toes," he corrected in the great British tradition.

"Baby to-may-toes," Kelly repeated, lengthening the long a. "Cherries, grapes, and apples," she added to complete the inventory. "Food's out. Come 'n' get it!"

They finished every scrap, leaving only some wine and fruit for dessert.

"I imagine you've done this quite a lot," Deil mused, lying flat on his back and squinting up at the sky.

"Done what?" Kelly was stretched out at a right angle to him, her head resting on his chest.

He lifted his right hand, which held a paper cup. "Come up here with a bottle of wine . . ."

"A loaf of bread and thee?" she poetically enumerated.

"I was thinking of Barry, actually."

"Barry," she chortled. "On a picnic? You must be kidding."

"Not the picnic type, eh?"

"Most assuredly not," she mimicked in precise tones, and was given a pinch for doing so.

"I thought you said Barry loved these mountains."

"He does. Or maybe it's lust and not love," she mused.

"How can you lust after a mountain? No"—Deil lifted his left hand to cover her half-open mouth—"don't tell me. I can see that gleam in your eyes!" She batted them at him. "You don't have to say a word."

"You're so perceptive," she teased once he'd removed his hand, trailing it down her cheek to rest on the base of her throat. "I meant that Barry's interest in these mountains is active. He hikes through them, skis down them, hurdles around them on a bike, jumps off them with a hang glider, or four-wheels all over them."

"Four-wheels?"

"In a jeep."

"You don't approve?"

"It disturbs the wildlife and I don't like all that jiggling."

"I don't know," Deil mused with roguish humor. "A little jiggle now and then might be nice."

Kelly threatened him with the ice cube still resting in her paper cup before saying, "Where was I? Oh, yes, Barry. He's never simply contemplated the mountains, enjoyed them. It's too . . . passive."

"Passive," Deil huffily repeated, his chest rising and

121

falling in feigned agitation, almost knocking Kelly's head off her resting place. "Is that what you're accusing me of?"

"Would I do a thing like that?" she innocently denied

"How about a thing like this?" he suggested, setting down his cup, and hers, so that he could grab her by the shoulders and tug her on top of him.

"Can I have five minutes to think about it?" she mockingly deliberated.

"I've told you," he retorted, his face a few inches from hers. "Humor won't work as a turn-off."

"Who's trying to turn you off?" she interrupted, her green eyes reflecting a decidedly come-hither look.

"It turns me on." He growled the warning.

"I can tell," she murmured, shifting her legs ever so slightly, the growing hardness of his male frame unmistakable.

He looked at her through half-closed lids. "You are a devilish tease!"

"Sure'n I'm a student of the *deil* himself!" Kelly's Scottish brogue held more enthusiasm than accuracy.

Deil stole the laughter from her lips. The kiss skipped over the teasing stage and went right into seductive deliberation, an evocative exchange of tongue-touched pleasures. By slightly changing the angle of his head, Deil gave the kiss a new slant and, as a result, a new level of enjoyment.

Resting as she was on the powerful length of his body, touching from head to toe, Kelly couldn't help but be aware of the taut state of his arousal. Their sensual proximity wrought havoc on her own nervous system, until she felt as if she were burning up inside. In the heat of the moment she grew impatient with their barrier of clothing, wanting to rip it away, yet unwilling to break their near-intimate contact for even the brief moment required to do so.

It took the shouted catcalls of a group of nearby hikers to draw them apart. Kelly silently seconded Deil's softly muttered oaths while trying to regain her breath.

"I can see I'm going to have to enroll in some course for stress management," he decided once they'd quickly repacked the rucksack. Unfulfilled passion still embered in his hazel eyes, warning of his barely restrained emotions.

Kelly tried to interject a measure of humor, momentarily forgetting its stimulating effect. "Barry used to get tanked."

"I'm high enough, thanks."

"No, I meant he'd go into those fiber glass flotation tanks for planned relaxation."

Deil shook his head in disbelief. "Only in Aspen . . ."

"That's not true," she pertly contradicted. "I'm sure there are similiar things elsewhere in the world."

On the return trip Kelly stopped to climb onto the time-worn surface of a dead tree. Some kind of birch, its pale bark had been honed to a polished smoothness. Kelly sat astride the suspended limb, as if it were a toy horse.

Deil unhitched his rucksack and followed suit, but not bestriding behind or in front of her as she'd expected. Instead he got on facing her, their noses almost touching.

"You're headed in the wrong direction," she breathlessly informed him.

"No, I'm not." His voice was low and intimate.

Bracing his feet against the dusty ground, he reached out to lift her legs. Kelly clung onto his shoulders in alarm, her sense of balance momentarily out of kilter. Deil pulled her close, hooking her knees up over his thighs. Releasing her stranglehold on his shoulders, Kelly slipped her arms around his waist. Her fingers threaded through the belt loops on the back of his jeans, her thumbs dipping into the waistband to caress the small of his back.

Random kisses were dropped across the plains of her face, from temple to jaw and back again. Deil's hands joined in the skilled seduction as he tantalizingly placed them in the back pocket of her jeans, molding her curvaceous form even closer. Pressed against the cradle of his masculinity, Kelly was aflame with desire. She'd awakened a sleeping tiger with her earlier flirtatiousness, and its passionate claws were ripping through them both.

"Still think I'm headed in the wrong direction?" he rasped against her lips.

"Who's thinking?" she whispered, resuming their kiss.

His lips molded her mouth as his hands molded her body, moving against her with wicked pleasure. Kelly's breathing was shallow and unsteady, her need for oxygen supplanted by her need for Deil. Her lips eagerly clung to his—parting, teasing, tasting, testing—and loving every moment of it!

Powerful spasms of excitation rocked them both, fanning the conflagrant friction of denim rubbing against denim. Beneath her legs the muscles of his thighs were rock hard, and as for the rest of his lower torso . . . Her thoughts swam. The pulsating beat of desire was an erotic metronome to the most sexually stimulating embrace Kelly had ever encountered, annihilating all preconceived ideas of what this could be like.

Once more it was the sound of catcalls from the same

bunch of hikers that brought them apart, as luck would have it. "At it again, you two?"

"Damn!" Deil uttered a groan of frustration. "That's twice we've almost gone over the edge in one day. Third time, watch out!"

CHAPTER EIGHT

"Flash, ahh . . . ahh . . . he'll save every one of us!" Kelly gustily sang along with a Queen album.

"Earth to cook, are you receiving?" Deil poked his head around the kitchen doorframe to inquire.

"Only compliments," she retorted with a wave of her vegetable peeler.

"Then I won't tell you the meat's burning."

"Oh, no!" Kelly frantically tried to salvage the meat from requiring carbon dating!

"Careful," Deil cautioned as she forgot to use a pot holder. "Don't hurt yourself."

"I'd like to hurt you," she countered. "Why didn't you tell me it was burning?"

"I called in to you, but you were singing at the top of your lungs and couldn't hear me."

"I was not singing at the top of my lungs. That was backup singing."

"If you say so."

"I do. Go on." She affectionately gave him a backward shove. "Go change the record."

"What do you want to hear next?" His question was yelled across the living room.

"Tug of War," Kelly yelled back, naming Paul McCartney's classic album.

"Don't you ever get tired of listening to that record?"

"Tired of Paul McCartney?" Her horrified voice came from the kitchen. "Blasphemy!"

"Remind me to tell you sometime about the press party I was invited to for Paul."

Kelly immediately stuck her head around the doorway to cry, "You actually met him?"

"I thought that might get your attention."

"Well?" she impatiently demanded. "Did you or didn't you?"

"Did I or didn't I what?" he asked with assumed perplexity.

"Don't give me that wide-eyed look. That devilish gleam in your eyes gives you away every time. I'm going to throw a frying pan at you in a minute!"

"I'll tell you after dinner. Meanwhile, I think something's burning again."

"You drive me crazy!" Kelly angrily avowed before returning to the kitchen to check on her culinary project.

Deil strolled in to join her a few minutes later. "It's awful quiet in here," he teased. "I've come to see what's wrong. Silence isn't a natural state for you!"

"Very funny," she sniffed, wiping her damp cheek with the back of her hand.

He reached out and caught a teardrop on the tip of his finger. "You're crying." Gathering her into a comforting embrace, he softly queried, "What's wrong?"

"I'm peeling onions." Kelly grinned at him through her tears. "For the Irish stew."

"So all this," he loosened his clasp, "was for nothing?"

"Oh, I wouldn't say that," Kelly provocatively protested. "It felt pretty good to me!"

"And you feel pretty good to me," he countered, deftly slipping his hand under the thin cotton of her shirt.

"So tell me"—she swirled her finger into intricate spirals behind his ear—"did you really meet Paul?"

"Almost." His voice was husky.

Kelly's voice was equally so as she repeated, "Almost?"

"Paul did show up at the party, but I didn't. I had the flu."

"We're going to have to stop this," she muttered against his lips.

"Why?" he muttered back. "Just because I didn't go to that party?"

Kelly laughed at his aggrieved tone. "No, because I don't want to burn anything again. Tonight I'm going to amaze you with my culinary skills."

The dinner did turn out to be delicious, her mother's recipe having stood her in good stead. Afterward Deil plied her with kisses more intoxicating than any after dinner liqueur. Lying in her lonely bed later that night, unable to sleep, Kelly was forced to diagnose her feelings for Deil as being a definite case of love. In the darkness she was able to look back and view the succession of emotions that had brought her to this point. Although she felt as though she'd been struck without warning, actually the opposite was true. There had been warning, there had been signs, but she'd been blind to them.

On the very first night he'd stayed at the apartment, she remembered, she'd felt the rumblings of physical attraction. Then, as she got to know Deil, she'd enjoyed their teasing, taunting conversations. The seeds of attraction grew, and were soon reflected in the meaningful glances, the flirtatious tone of their bantering.

As for Deil's feelings for her, Kelly knew he was attracted to her, knew he cared about her. But she also knew his experience with Fiona had left him gun-shy. It would be up to her to prove how unalike she and Fiona were.

The thought of Fiona's romantic presumptions was what had restrained Kelly from rocking the boat. She had no moral qualms about wanting to go to bed with Deil; she loved him and was certain of that love. But she was also realistic enough to know that he was serious in his intention of remaining single. Furthermore, she had no rose-tinted delusions about being the one woman who could change his mind.

At twenty-seven, she knew that love frequently wasn't enough for a lifetime commitment, there were other more practical considerations to be made. Kelly was walking into this relationship with her eyes open. Armed with that self-realization, she determined to make a move soon. Any more sleepless nights like tonight and she'd be a basket case!

Her opportunity came the very next day. Glancing at the oversize calendar adorning the kitchen wall, she saw a near illegible note in Sally's scrawl. "Deil's B-day" Kelly translated. And it was on Saturday, the twenty-third. Only two days away. Perfect!

"Kelly, why is there a linen towel from the Mayo Clinic in our bathroom?" Deil demanded from the hallway.

"Been reading again, have you?" she jauntily returned, admiring the way his green polo shirt heightened the green flecks in his hazel eyes. He looked confidently attractive, warmly alive, and damn sexy!

"Last week it was the Hilton Hotel, now the Mayo

Clinic. My dear Watson, could this be the case of the kleptomaniac visitor?"

"I give up." Deciding not to tell him that she'd picked the towels up at a flea market, Kelly widened her eyes in pretended awe. "Could it?"

Deil cupped an imaginary pipe and then murmured, "Hmmm, this looks like a case for Sherlock Holmes."

"Unfortunately he's unavailable, so I guess I'll just have to make do with you, English!"

"Make do?" he moved closer to challenge.

"Make love?" Damn, she'd done it again, spilling her thoughts instead of considering them carefully before speaking.

The air was suddenly taut with sexual electricity. Vividly reactive current rushed between them, springing from expressive eyes to racing hearts. It wouldn't have surprised Kelly one bit if that current alone hadn't set off the telephone bell; it was certainly powerful enough! But the ringing was authentic, a long-distance call from Sally.

"Sally? Where are you?" Kelly asked the moment she heard her friend's voice.

"I'm still in London." Sally briefly listed some of her activities before saying, "Oh, Kelly, it's good to talk to you. I was afraid you might not be speaking to me."

"I was a little surprised by your arrangements."

"Still friends?"

"Still friends," Kelly assured.

"How's my flat?" Deil demanded in the background.

"What's that?" Kelly spoke into the receiver. "You've sold all your brother's furniture and blown the money? Way to go, Sally!"

Deil grabbed the phone away from Kelly. "What have you done?" he bellowed at his sister, who was relieved to be several thousand miles away if his voice was anything to go by.

"I haven't done anything. At least, not yet," Sally amended.

"Good. Then don't."

"Deil . . ."

"You're not to sell one stick of my furniture!"

"Deil . . ."

"Is that understood?" he demanded with typical big-brother dominance.

"Deil, will you shut up about your stupid furniture!" Sally's voice held an equal amount of sisterly impatience. "Kelly was only teasing you."

"Only teasing, was she?" The quelling look he bestowed on Kelly promised retribution.

"Deil, I'm thinking of getting married," Sally relayed in a breathless rush.

That got his attention. "Married? You're kidding, I hope?"

"It's no joking matter."

"Do I know the guy?"

"He's your next-door neighbor, as a matter of fact."

"Tristian? But he's married."

"Not Tristian, Andrew."

"You wouldn't be talking about Prince Andrew?"

"Of course not," Sally snapped in exasperation. "He's not a neighbor of yours."

"Then you must be talking about Andrew Denton."

"That's right."

"Sally, Andrew Denton is . . . He's a cold fish."

"Not with me he's not!"

"Do you know what he does for a living?"

"He's a librarian."

"Right. A librarian." Deil made it sound like the ultimate insult.

"So?"

"So, you know what they say about male librarians."

"No, I don't, actually, and I don't care to. For a supposedly intelligent man, you're not making much sense, brother dear. You don't approve of Andrew because of what 'they say' about librarians? I'm disappointed in you. Put Kelly back on the line," she peremptorily ordered. "Maybe she'll be more coherent than you seem to be."

"I'm perfectly coherent, thank you," Deil grated.

"You're welcome," she returned with pseudo-politeness.

"Sally, don't rush into anything," he cautioned.

"Rushing does not run in our family," she reminded him.

"I never thought it did." His tone held a certain ambiguousness.

"Sounds like you've been tempted to do a bit of rushing yourself, brother dear. How are things going between you and Kelly? She's beautiful, isn't she?"

"Yes, she is, but that's not the point." Deil was painfully aware of his sister's matchmaking—it had strained their sibling relationship once before. "We were talking about you and Denton."

"No, we weren't," Sally corrected. "I was done talking about Andrew and you were lecturing me about it!"

"Does this mean you won't be coming back here in September?" Deil noted Kelly's start of surprise upon hearing him voice the question.

"I haven't decided yet. Andrew's asked me to move in with him."

"Move in with him?" Deil growled in anger.

132

"You sound disapproving."

"I am."

"But you're living with Kelly."

"That's different," he dismissed.

"Still? I thought you'd surely have made a move by now. You're not letting that bad experience you had with Fiona stand in your way, are you?" Her voice became serious. "Part of that was my fault; I thought it was time you got married."

"And you no longer do?"

"I'm older and wiser now. I'm not so quick to wish you on my friends!"

"And I am not about to discuss the details of my private life with you."

"Good. That usually means there are some details to discuss. I'll return the favor and I won't discuss my private life with you. Just wanted to let you know that everything here is going well. Your plants look healthier than when I arrived, and Andrew fixed the leaky bathroom faucet. Give my love to Kelly. Gotta go. I'll talk to you again soon. Cheerio!"

Deil stared at the buzzing receiver in disgusted impatience before slamming it down on the cradle.

"What was all that about?" Kelly demanded. "Did you say something about Sally not coming back in September?"

"You of all people should know how scatterbrained my sister can be. She's met some man and is thinking of marriage."

"I see." While Kelly was pleased on Sally's behalf, she was also worried on her own. She'd never be able to afford to keep the apartment on her own, which meant she'd have to find another roommate if Sally decided to stay in London.

Seeing her worried face, Deil's own expression softened. "Don't worry about it. Sally's just at the considering stage, nothing definite."

"For Sally to even reach the considering stage means it's pretty serious," she astutely observed. "But, as you say, there's no point worrying about it now. There's nothing I can do anyway, except wish her the best."

"It sure as hell wouldn't be fair for her to stick you with the lease for this place," Deil angrily protested.

"The way it wasn't fair for me to stick you with the bill at the restaurant," she countered with a dexterous change of subject.

"That was different. You didn't stick me, you tried paying me back."

"But you refused to accept. Which leaves me with only one option."

"Not the pork-chop threat again?" Deil looked suitably horrified at the very idea.

"Only as a last resort. I'll simply have to take you out to dinner again, and this time I'll be sure to bring my wallet."

"Sure," he accepted, glad to be let off so easily.

"Good, I'm pleased you agree."

"Would it matter if I didn't?" He lifted a mocking brow at her.

"Only in the short run," was her cryptic reply. "Then it's settled. I'll take you out for your birthday this Saturday."

"Wait a minute. How did you know Saturday's my birthday?"

"I have my sources," Kelly loftily informed him, her

green eyes full of mischievous laughter. "I also know the name of the stuffed dog you had as a kid—Ruffie, which finger you broke in the softball tournament—right hand pinkie."

"And do you know how old I'm going to be this birthday?"

"Thirty," she promptly answered.

"God, that sounds old!"

"So long as it doesn't *feel* old."

"I'm beginning to. Feel old, that is."

Kelly's amusement grew. "I have noticed you leaning rather heavily on your cane lately. Is the rheumatism worrying you again?" She patted his arm with exaggerated commiseration. "Never mind. Women sometimes go for 'older men.' " Whirling away, she avoided his threatening grip. "Gotta run! I'm supposed to be at the gallery in eight and a half minutes."

Kelly was late, although it was entirely Deil's fault for spending four of her allotted eight and a half minutes in kissing her! Not that she voiced a complaint; she wasn't left with enough breath to say anything. Which was just as well, as her thoughts were getting steamy again!

Saturday morning seemed like a long time coming. Kelly walked into the living room to find Deil sprawled on the couch, daily newspaper in hand. With a casual "Morning" she joined him at the opposite end of the couch, lifting her feet onto the cushions a few inches from his.

Deil murmured an absent reply, his attention monopolized by the staid gazette. Piqued by his preoccupation, Kelly set out to make her presence felt in the most literal sense of the word. Taking her cue from a nationally televised promotional campaign, she let her fingers do the walking, strolling up the seam of Deil's jeans. The inside seam! She didn't get much above his knee when she was shanghaied and heaved onto his chest.

"You're crushing *The New York Times,* English!"

"That's nothing compared to what you were doing to me," he growled.

"Really?" Her fingers crept inside the unbuttoned V of his shirt. "Tell me more."

"Maybe I should just show you."

"Maybe you should," she concurred, excited by the suggestively intimate quality of his low-toned offer.

Deil's lips brushed across hers with unerring precision. The kiss, while starting lightly, drew her into a heavy maelstrom of emotion. Differing slants of ever-questing mouths transformed their kisses into a mercurial kaleidoscope, blending passion, tenderness, affection, and desire into ever-changing configurations. For Kelly, no one else's kisses had ever been as all-encompassing. With Deil the lightest touch became something special, something unique.

Feeling the corner of something hard pressing against the back of his neck, Deil huskily murmured, "What have you got in your hand?" without lifting his lips from hers.

Kelly lifted drooping eyelids, unable to focus because of his nearness. "Hand?"

"Hand," he leaned away to repeat with mocking humor. "Attached to end of arm, holding something hard."

"Oh, that." She unclasped her arms from around his neck, lowering her hand to reveal a small, wrapped package. "It's a birthday present for you. Many happy returns!"

"So long as they're unaudited returns, I'll be happy!"

Kelly groaned her protest before countering, "Are you sure you're not an undercover agent for the IRS?" She held the present just out of his reach, awaiting his reply. "I mean, the way you were able to organize my bills was nothing short of miraculous."

"Another one of my . . ."

". . . many talents." She completed the sentence for him. "So you've told me. Maybe I should make you my business manager," she mused.

"I'd want 100 percent."

"Of my unmade millions?"

"Of your body!" he leered.

"Done!" Kelly promptly accepted, grinning as he blinked in surprise.

Recovering quickly, he intimately promised, "Not yet, but soon."

Not to be outdone, she whispered, "I hope so," and then laughed. Laughed at the warmth of their physical and visual contact, laughed with the sheer happiness of being close to the man she loved. "Here." She thrust the small gift into his hands, retreating slightly so he could open it.

Deil shook the present first, but the slight rattling noise told him little aside from the fact that the box wasn't empty. He began unwrapping the fancy paper with the same kind of deliberate efficiency he applied to any task. None of the wild ripping and tearing Kelly indulged in!

"What are you smiling at?" he demanded with an element of wariness. "Is this present booby-trapped or something?"

"What a suspicious mind you have," she reprimanded him. "You've been reading too many Sherlock Holmes books. We're in Aspen, not on Baker Street."

Deil removed the paper to stare in momentary astonishment and delight at the universal amusement in his hand. "Crayons!"

Kelly was relieved at his pleasure, she wasn't sure he'd see the humor in the whimsical gift. "I thought it was time you deserved a new box of crayons."

Deil opened the box and sniffed. "They even smell the same."

"Of course they do."

"This really brings back memories." He smiled nostalgically. "My first writing assignments were done with crayons, on the bathroom wall if I recall correctly. My mother was not amused."

"I'm sure she wasn't. What did you write?"

"The entire alphabet."

"I'm impressed. To show such promise at that early age."

"I was fourteen," Deil replied with such a straight face that Kelly almost fell for it.

"You were?"

Her solicitous gaze made him crack up, ruining his con game.

"You're awful!" she accused.

"So my mother told me."

"Your mother sounds like an excellent judge of character."

"That she is. Too bad it didn't wipe off on her son."

"How do you know it didn't?"

"Because, if I'd have been a good judge of character, I would've spotted Fiona a mile away."

"Everyone is entitled to a few mistakes. I had David; you had Fiona. You can't let your mistakes warp your outlook on life."

"My outlook isn't warped. Let's just say I'm naturally skeptical."

"That's an understatement."

"You're not supposed to insult the birthday boy," Deil drawled.

"Boy?" she questioned. "At thirty?"

"Blame it on the crayons; they've brought out the child in me."

"Just don't start writing on these walls," she sternly decreed.

"Cute. Very cute."

Kelly was once more tumbled forward through the V of his legs for another romantic romp. It was some time before they came back to earth and mundane things like eating.

"You never told me where you're taking me for dinner." Deil settled her firmly beside him, a safe distance away.

Kelly smiled knowingly, well aware of Deil's reason for small talk. They'd been too close a moment ago for her not to know. "I thought I'd splurge and take you to McDonalds." Her voice reflected the same playful anticipation gleaming in her eyes.

"A McDonald's? In Aspen? No way!"

"Well, then, would you believe an early supper at . . ." Kelly named one of Aspen's better restaurants, well known for its romantic ambience.

"That I'd believe. Tonight promises to be a most enjoyable evening."

"It will be!" There was no doubt in her mind.

Kelly's limited wardrobe didn't hold two dresses fancy enough for an evening out, so she had to wear her sea green silk again. Its simple style allowed for variations in accessories that gave it enormous versatility. Tonight a stunning necklace of raw turquoise and a matching inlaid belt gave the dress an entirely new look. Her strappy sandals again brought her up to Deil's height.

He was wearing his suit with a lightweight shirt in deference to the summer heat. The burgundy-colored tie was the same one Kelly had slipped from around his neck the night of the fireworks display. His hair had gotten longer in the intervening two and a half weeks, and it gave him a rakish handsomeness that she found infinitely appealing and utterly sexy.

Kelly was none too pleased that their beautiful waitress felt the same! Openly flirting with Deil, she leaned across him to reveal her generous proportions while serving them. After one particularly obvious come-on, Kelly was tempted to trip the waitress, restraining herself only with difficulty.

"Shall I warn her that her life is in peril?" Deil solemnly inquired.

Kelly returned her gaze to him. "I beg your pardon?"

"Kelly you've been throwing dangerous looks at our gregarious waitress all evening."

"And she's been throwing herself across you all evening."

"Has she? I hadn't noticed. I've been too wrapped up in you to notice anything else."

His mention of wrapping brought to mind the way his lean fingers had carefully undone the colorful paper covering his presents. In addition to the box of crayons, she'd also given him a mystery from the best-seller list and a stained glass replica of a violin, Sherlock Holmes's instrument.

Each present had been unwrapped with meticulous

care, and Kelly couldn't help noticing that Deil used that same care with relationships, not blindly ripping and tearing, but slowly uncovering whatever concealment Kelly had erected until he'd gotten to know the real her, gotten to the very heart of her. And if one applied the same technique toward making love, the outcome was sure to be ravishingly pleasurable.

Deil insisted on paying for the specially selected champagne, toasting her with his eyes as well as his glass. Kelly couldn't remember what she ordered, or what it tasted like; all she could think about was returning to the apartment and giving Deil his last present, the most personal one of all.

They arrived at the apartment relatively early, shortly after ten. In view of the warmly responsive looks they'd exchanged all evening, Deil was stunned when Kelly murmured "Good night" and went into her room, closing the door behind her. He almost followed her, and to hell with the cramped confines of the single beds occupying each bedroom! He wanted to make love to his seductive roommate all night long, not simply grab a quick bit of fun and retire to his own cold bed. Swearing softly, yet with vehement impatience, Deil tugged off his tie and headed for a cold shower.

Kelly's soft voice called to him just as he finished brushing his teeth. "Deil?"

He opened the bathroom door, but she wasn't in the hallway. He followed her voice to the living room and found her sitting in the middle of what looked like a huge double bed.

"Where did that bed come from?" he heard himself ask.

"Is that all you can think about?" Kelly purred the

challenge, her eyes beckoning to him, her kimonoed figure bathed by the moonlight pouring in from the generous bay windows.

"No, you're all I can think about."

"I'm going to bed, Deil."

He recognized their special phrase at once. "Is that an invitation?"

"Yes, it most definitely is."

"Hallelujah!" He joined her on the bed, his legs and feet bare beneath the short blue terry robe. "I could strangle you for not telling me this was a sofa bed. Don't you know that I've been lying awake nights trying to figure a way of getting my hands on a bed big enough for both of us?" While he spoke, his hand glided up her arm, over the curve of her shoulder, and around to her back.

"You never said anything."

"Didn't I?" he growled. "I thought you knew."

Kelly leaned forward to place a remorseful kiss on Deil's bared collarbone, a promising token of love.

Meanwhile his exploring hand had completed its reconnaissance of her back and made a tantalizing discovery. "You're not wearing anything under this kimono!"

"Surprised?" she husked, sliding her own hands down the warm wall of his chest.

"Delighted," he corrected, consummately untying the restraining belt and unwrapping her, just as she'd imagined him doing, with infinite care and sensuous deliberation.

Deil checked her eyes for final confirmation before sliding the kimono from her shoulders, disclosing the feminine richness of her beauty. She was a study of soft curves and warm valleys, her skin sensuously gleaming from the

142

moon's silvery light. Slowly, surely, he completely un-draped her, casting off her robe and then his own.

For her part, Kelly gloried in giving her ultimate gift with passionate generosity, offering of herself without reservation. She wasn't a sacrificial offering, nor a Lady Bountiful dispensing favors. No; she was a woman in love, determined to share this final intimacy with the man she loved.

Kelly heard and felt his indrawn breath at the touch of her fingers on his warm skin. Her hands acted like tiny sensors on an exploratory trip to a new planet, recording information before sending it back to the brain for evalua-tion. She marveled at his hidden strength, of tanned skin stretched over rippling muscles and unyielding bone.

"You've got capable hands," Deil breathed.

"Capable?" she pouted, becoming more daring in her investigation.

"Umm," he groaned, moving against her, drawing her down onto the uncluttered confines of the bed. "Capable of driving me crazy!"

His lips caught hers, temporarily stilling the teasing kisses she was showering across his face. The touch of his mouth was intoxicating, addictive, feeding her deep-seat-ed needs, a tantalizing appetizer that only left her hungry for more. Her brain was saturated with sensual input—the minty taste of his toothpaste, the tangy scent of his soap, the silken roughness of his skin, the harsh unevenness of his breathing.

Deil's hands pressed the small of her back to slowly draw her into his embrace like a fisherman reeling in his catch, until she was evocatively molded against the warmth of his powerful body. His locked hands then rose to press her upper torso against his. The erogenous radiance of his embrace was dazzling.

His lips strayed for a leisurely inspection of her temples, meandering across her cheeks to play at the corners of her mouth until she blindly turned her head, her parted lips intercepting his. The kiss consumed her, voracious in its adoration. The sweeter her responses became, the more he wanted to taste their honey.

The magic of Deil's kiss blended with the sensual pleasure of his touch. His hands were moving again, rolling down her back to her waist and lower before rolling back up again, advancing and retreating like an erotic wave. Her nerves were honeycombed with the impetus, each cell's individual receptors tingling simultaneously.

Her fingers grazed over his back, registering his moan of pleasure with a heady sense of power. Kelly did whatever came naturally, her uninhibitedness stealing Deil's breath and occasionally his composure. Her nimble fingers stroked the firm lines of his body, intent on returning some of the thrilling excitement he was provoking.

Deil communicated his pleasure, sharing it with her and thereby compounding it. The auditory stimulation of his intimate promises and impassioned compliments opened up another avenue of seduction. It was an avenue that was impudently explored, making them equal partners in the collaborative art of making love.

Kelly shivered uncontrollably as his fingertips skimmed her curves and hollows with erotic delicacy, covering her from head to toe. The ceaseless current singing in her veins intensified its insistent song. Deil's skillful hands read her like a book—studying, teaching, learning her erogenous zones. Those questing hands registered the fluctuating explosions they'd so lovingly triggered before instigating more. Moving through revolving doors of intense pleasure, she was blinded by the exhilarating pace.

His lips reached down to whisper in her ear, "Slowly, honey, slowly," his voice hoarse with control, but Kelly was past understanding. She mindlessly caught him to her, her fiery touch shattering his slipping control. Deil gathered her in, his penetration of the pain-guarded, pleasure-coated passage accomplished with stunning passion.

Waves of feverish desire continued to roll over her with demanding persistence. Propulsive power shot through her, lifting her up to a dizzying peak of jubilant enlightenment until their bodies swayed in time to that inner rhythm. The sublime motion slowed as they entered another dimension of desire, one that changed time, lengthening it, at times even suspending it altogether, only to have it rush back in a free fall through the sudden darkness, showering them both with the oscillating embers.

CHAPTER NINE

"How do you feel?" Deil's voice was husky with remembered passion.

Kelly drowsily rubbed her cheek against his bare chest. "Like I've died and gone to heaven!"

For several moments Deil made no reply, but when he did speak, it was to say, "Would you mind coming back to earth? I want to talk to you."

He sounded serious, too serious, so she teased him. "I thought men didn't like to talk afterward."

Her efforts to lighten his mood didn't work. "I'd hardly say you're an expert on the subject. Why didn't you tell me you were a virgin?" he demanded.

Her bare shoulders lifted in a shrug. "You never asked."

"The question never occurred to me." His voice held a mixture of dry derisiveness and satirical self-reflection. "Your behavior has never been that of a shy novice."

Kelly took his remark to be a compliment, even though she wasn't sure it was offered as one. "Why, thank you."

"You always seemed to be with me all the way," he mused, almost to himself.

"I was. It was beautiful!" Her voice was a satisfied purr as she nestled closer.

"You're a very passionate woman. Why didn't you ever sleep with Luce? Or David?"

Kelly stiffened at the sound of David's name. "Would you have preferred that I did?"

Deil's expression tightened. "No."

"Then leave well enough alone," she advised, getting up from the bed and donning her kimono.

"Why me?" Deil persisted, sitting up in bed.

"I'm choosy."

He combed an angry hand through his tousled hair. "Damn it, Kelly, this isn't a peanut butter commercial! Why choose me? Why give me your virginity?"

"I didn't plan on keeping it for the rest of my life," Kelly tartly countered, resenting this third degree.

"Kelly." Her name came out as a threatening growl. "I want the truth."

"What are you so concerned about?" she flared. "That I'm going to pull a 'Fiona' on you and try trapping you into marriage?"

The look on Deil's face was confirmation enough.

"Then let me quickly allay your fears. I'm on the pill; there isn't any danger of pregnancy. You may have found me somewhat lacking in experience, but I'm not uneducated!" she scathingly stated.

"I never thought you were," he quietly denied, rubbing his hand against his jaw in the manner of a man who'd gotten more than he'd bargained for and knew he had to proceed with caution. "I'm trying to figure out what makes you tick, what made you keep all your fiery emotions on hold. I've told you why I've been so cautious about starting a relationship with you. What's your excuse?"

147

"You're not the only one recovering from a rotten relationship, you know."

"I realize that. Talk to me. Tell me about it."

The eloquent persuasion of his voice lessened Kelly's anger, and her inherent honesty came to the fore. "I already told you about David's rotten behavior. What I didn't tell you was that we were on the verge of sleeping together when I had my skiing accident. It shook me to realize how close I'd come to making an utter fool of myself. I was never tempted to take a chance again, until I met you. Then I knew, hard though it was to accept. Knew that I loved you," she ended in an uncharacteristic rush.

"Oh, Kelly—"

"That doesn't mean I want to marry you," she fiercely interrupted. "What you seem to be forgetting is that I've got my own career to think about, and it's every bit as important to me as your writing is to you."

"You do realize I've got to go back to London soon. I've got only a little over a month left."

"I know," Kelly sighed in angry exasperation. "Would you stop worrying that I'm going to tie you down or take away your freedom? What do I have to do to convince you? Sign a sworn affidavit?"

"I'm sorry." Deil wearily thrust one hand through the casual disorder of his hair, sending the wavy strands tumbling over his forehead. "I was jumping to conclusions, something a good journalist should never do. There were mitigating circumstances however."

"You already told me about Fiona."

"She wasn't the only mistake I've made. Suffice it to say that I've been burned more than once."

"So have I. Isn't it time we both stopped looking back?"

148

"I suppose it is." His voice softened magically. "It's also time for me to tell you that I love you."

Her eyes widened in apparent amazement. "You do?" Deil had said he liked her, wanted her, but he'd never used the word *love* before.

"You don't have to sound so surprised about it. I do love you, Kelly. I have for some time. But I never said anything because . . ." His explanation trailed off.

"You were afraid I'd equate love with marriage," she guessed.

"Most people do."

"I'm not most people."

"You certainly aren't. You're someone very special. You're the woman I love. Now, why don't you come back to bed so I can show you just how special you are, and how very much I love you." He reached out and hooked her in his embrace.

"My, what long arms you have!" Kelly marveled, her heart singing with the joyful knowledge of his love.

"All the better to hold you, my dear Watson," he misquoted the Big Bad Wolf.

She allowed herself to be pulled back onto the bed. "I always knew you were a wolf."

"In sheep's clothing?" he queried, opening her kimono to caress the full softness of her breasts.

"In no clothing at all!" she murmured, seductively entangling her bare limbs with his.

They lay together in the mellow aftermath of making love, their bodies relaxed, their voices hushed. This was the time to reveal thoughts, share confidences.

Deil began. "What was the first thing you noticed about

me?" He listened to her reply in astonished silence before protesting, "I am not skinny!"

"I said you looked skinny," Kelly corrected. "But you feel just right." Her fingers strolled along his rib cage, skirting the area between the fourth and fifth ribs because she knew that's where he was ticklish. "Don't you know the story of Goldilocks and the Three Bears?"

"Are you going to tell me a bedtime story?" he growled, ensnaring her fingers.

Kelly grinned and shook her head. "What was the first thing you noticed about me?"

"That you were kicking me out of your apartment," he promptly replied.

"Besides that."

He eyed her with deliberate intent, his gaze as provocative as a touch. "Then I guess I'd have to say it was a toss-up between your body and your eyes."

"Speaking of eyes . . ." She feathered a finger across his arched brows. "Are you still wearing your contacts?"

"Oh, my God, I left them in the bathroom when you called! Don't let me forget they're there. Otherwise I might knock them down the drain or something!"

"Do you remember the night you lost one lens on the bedroom floor?" she reminisced.

"Do I ever. You were saved by the bell."

"I didn't feel saved at the time."

"No?"

"No."

"What did you feel like at the time?" His voice lowered to a husky resonance.

"Like doing this." She suited her words with action and they were once more caught up in the beckoning labyrinth of love.

Kelly's happiness was complete. With her usual determination she resolved not to worry about the future, to take each day as it came, and enjoy it to the fullest. If her time with Deil was to be short in quantity, it would be great in quality! There would be time enough to cry after he left.

Although Kelly had always enjoyed Deil's company, now that they were lovers she felt a very special contentment in his presence, a magical satisfaction. Simple things like taking a bath suddenly became pleasurable diversions when shared.

Their bathtub was a cast-iron original. Deil claimed that the building's owners must have run out of renovating money by the time they got to the bathroom, but Kelly suggested that the bathtub had been deliberately purchased to match the Victorian decor of the apartment. Either way, its grandiose size mocked the cramped smallness of the bathroom itself.

Because the apartment wasn't air-conditioned, Kelly was wearing a pair of khaki shorts and a red halter. Deil, who was preparing to take a bath, soon wore nothing at all!

"What was this before renovation? Another closet?" he growled in complaint after stubbing his toe.

"A water closet, perhaps?" she laughed.

Kelly's admiring gaze lingered on him, for she never tired of looking at his body, her artist's eye appreciating the long line of leg and torso while her libido appreciated all the parts in between!

He settled into the waiting tub. "The water's fine. Why don't you join me?"

"Okay, I will!" Kelly didn't even bother removing her clothes, she simply stepped in and sat down, laughing at

Deil's look of surprise. "You shouldn't issue invitations if you're not serious."

"Oh, I am serious." He pulled her close, possessively holding her to him, guiding her mouth to his. The kiss was a passionate vehicle for the expression of their love, as were the fevered caresses both were exchanging.

"Damn!" Deil swore as his elbow hit the bathtub's cast iron side. "A tub is fine for bathing and fooling around, but for the serious stuff I prefer a bed, even if it is a hidden one!"

Hauling her up with him, he swiftly removed her soggy clothes and then wrapped a bath sheet around the both of them. Kelly was then frog-marched into the living room, where pillows were stripped from the sofa and tossed helter-skelter across the floor. As soon as the bed was unfolded they fell onto its firm mattress in a damp heap of warmly entangled limbs.

Unfortunately they were promptly interrupted by a sudden knocking on the apartment door.

"Don't answer," Deil huskily advised. "Whoever it is will have to come back later." His teeth gently assaulted her ear with maddening little nibbles. "Much later. Next week, maybe!"

"Come on! I know someone's home. Open up!" The knocking turned into insistent hammering.

"Tom!" Kelly broke away to exclaim.

"You know that maniac?" Deil was surprised.

"That maniac is my brother."

"I thought you said your brother's name was Larry."

"That's another brother."

"How many do you have, for God's sake?"

"Four."

"Almost enough for a regiment," Deil muttered.

"You sound like you're about to face a firing squad."

"And your brother sounds like he's about to kick the door down," Deil retorted dryly. "You'd better let him in."

"I'm coming!" Kelly yelled for her brother's benefit before whispering to Deil, "We've got to get dressed! And get this bed folded up!"

"Is this brother older or younger than you are?" Deil inquired, getting up from the bed as if he had all the time in the world.

"Younger." Kelly jammed the cushions back on the bedframe the moment it was folded. "Why?"

"I just wanted to know if I was in for a lecture from a stern older brother."

"Tom's only nineteen." Then she turned to yell "I'll be there in a second!" as her brother resumed his pounding.

Deil confidently ambled off toward his room while Kelly scurried into hers to grab an Indian cotton kaftan from the back of the door. Its looseness would conceal the fact that she wore nothing beneath it, a situation she'd have to remedy later. Racing back to the living room, she paused a second to smooth her hair and catch her breath before opening the door. "Tom! What a surprise!"

"What took you so long?" he complained, stepping into the room.

"I was in the shower," she fabricated. "What are you doing here?"

"Didn't you get my letter?" Tom asked, slinging his beat-up backpack onto the floor.

"No."

"I gave it to a truck driver in New Mexico."

"Without a stamp, if I know you." Kelly shook her head in exasperation. Tom was hitchhiking his way across

153

the country, much to their mother's dismay. Kelly had suspected that he'd drop by when he got to Colorado, but had not heard from him. Now he was returning back east to resume college in September. Of all her brothers Tom was the most unpredictable and the most boisterous.

"So where's your roommate?" He looked around with unconcealed curiosity.

"He's in his room."

"He?" Tom's sandy eyebrows rose several inches.

"Sally's brother."

"Where's Sally?"

"In London," Kelly replied as Deil walked into the room, respectfully dressed in a pair of jeans and a T-shirt.

Kelly made the introductions. "Deil, I'd like you to meet Tom, my baby brother."

Deil eyed the young man's 6 foot 4 inch frame in amusement while shaking his offered hand. "If you're the baby, I'd be afraid to meet the oldest!"

Tom grinned, accustomed to such jokes about his height. "So are you just here for a visit or what?"

"Deil's visiting," she quickly interjected.

"Oh?" Tom's face wore an expression of friendly curiosity. "For how long?"

This time Deil answered for himself before Kelly could do so for him. "I'm going back to London at the end of the month."

"I wanted to go over to Europe this summer," Tom sighed, "but I ran out of bread."

"Tom's an impoverished student," Kelly explained.

"I remember the feeling," Deil sympathized.

"So that's why I've come to crash here." Tom turned to face Kelly. "You told me you had a Hide-a-bed I could use."

154

"That's right," she slowly confirmed, trying not to look as upset as she felt. "Uh, it's here in the living room."

"That'll be fine." Tom sat down on the couch and looked around with interest. He'd never visited his sister's apartment before. "I can stay only a few days though," he warned.

"A few days." Kelly and Deil spoke in unison, reflecting varying degrees of consternation.

Tom looked from one to the other. "Hey, I'm not breaking up anything, am I?"

"Of course not," Kelly quickly denied, slanting Deil a look that warned him not to contradict her.

"I've got a ride as far as Iowa, but the guy's not leaving until Wednesday," Tom explained.

"No problem," Kelly assured him with feigned certainty. "Would you like something to eat?"

"Always. Just head me toward the bathroom, so I can clean up first."

The moment Tom was out of the room, Deil grabbed Kelly's arm, preventing her from slipping off into the kitchen.

"I couldn't tell Tom the truth," she hastily defended herself, anticipating his complaint.

"Why not?"

"Because. Telling him would be like telling my mother. For all his 6 foot 4 he's still putty in my mother's hands when it comes to inquisition time."

"So what do you propose we do?" Deil impatiently demanded. "Resume the roles of platonic roommates?"

"Not exactly. Just act naturally."

"If I were to act naturally, I'd take you back to bed and keep you there," he huskily murmured.

"I want that too," she whispered back. "But I can't kick my own brother out. I haven't seen him in two years."

"I know. It's just rotten timing."

In appreciation for his understanding, Kelly bestowed a quick apologetic kiss. "Sorry."

She was even sorrier as she tossed and turned in her narrow single bed that night. No matter how she tried, she couldn't fall asleep, not without the warmth of Deil's body beside her. She missed him.

He's only in the next room, an inner voice mocked. *How are you going to cope when he's halfway across the world in London? How are you going to sleep then?* Repeating Scarlett O'Hara's words, she punched her pillow and muttered, "I'll think about that tomorrow."

The way Kelly saw it, she had two options. She could be miserable now, and waste the short time she had with Deil, or she could be miserable later. Of the two, she preferred the latter.

Monday was Kelly's day at the gallery. She brought her brother with her so that Deil could work uninterrupted at the apartment. Tom had been impressed with the compact word processor and was well-versed in the microtechnology that made its portable size possible.

"I like your roommate," Tom told her as they walked across Aspen's pedestrian mall. "If he's the one, I approve!"

"I'll keep that in mind. What do you think of Aspen?" she asked, eager to change the subject.

"It's not as bad as I thought it would be," Tom had to admit.

"You mean the streets aren't paved in gold and the sidewalks clogged with jet setters?"

Tom grinned somewhat sheepishly. "I guess that was

what I expected." He browsed around Artisans for a while, impressed by Kelly's recent work. "You've really improved, sis!" When the gallery got busy he left to explore the town on his own, promising to return to the apartment by four.

After a hectic morning filled with many customers, things finally slowed down just before lunchtime, giving Kelly the opportunity to call Deil. The line was busy, even though she tried several times. Ozzie, no doubt, talking to London again.

Bonnie came in at two to take over. But Kelly couldn't go home yet; she had work to catch up on in the studio, work that she'd already put off.

"My brother Tom is in town," Kelly told her friend. "Do you think you and Ivan might be able to come over to dinner so that you can meet him?"

"When?"

"Tom's leaving Wednesday morning, so it would have to be tonight or tomorrow night. His visit was unexpected, or I would've planned something ahead of time," Kelly apologetically explained.

"Tomorrow night we've got plans, but tonight would be fine. I'd love to get away from my M&M's for a while!"

Kelly had to smile at Bonnie's look of parental exasperation. "Is seven all right?"

"Should be. I'll phone Ivan and check with him." Bonnie did so right then and was still laughing when she hung up the phone. "Ivan's going crazy. Magda tried sticking the cat's tail in her mouth. But enough about my problems. How're things going between you and Deil?"

"Fine."

"Is he still going back to London at the end of the month?"

"Yes."

"Maybe you should go with him."

"I don't think so." Catching her friend's worried expression, Kelly said, "I'm fine. I know what I'm doing. There's no such thing as a free lunch, so I guess I'm eating now and paying later."

"So long as you don't get yourself into hock!"

Kelly reached Deil by phone a few minutes later to tell him about their dinner guests. "I tried calling you earlier, but the line was busy. Ozzie again?"

"Guilty as charged. What's for dinner?"

"I haven't got a clue. What do we have in the fridge?"

"Yogurt, peanut butter, and root beer," he listed.

"In that case I'd better do some grocery shopping."

"How about a rendezvous in the frozen foods section?"

"Are you serious?" she laughed.

"I'm desperate!" he dramatically groaned.

"What's wrong?" Kelly's inflection was warmly teasing. "Haven't you read a paper today?"

"I haven't read you today." His voice reached out through the phone line to stroke her senses.

Kelly dreamily fingered the receiver, wishing it were Deil's warm flesh she was touching and not cool plastic. "I'll meet you in fifteen minutes," she softly promised. "The frozen foods section."

A short time later she wondered at the appropriateness of their meeting spot. Dressed in a wraparound cotton skirt and a sleeveless tunic top, her bare arms and legs were both sporting goosebumps caused by the combination of the supermarket's air-conditioning and the frigid air emanating from the open freezers behind her. She was vigorously rubbing her hands up and down her arms when another hand joined hers. Recognizing his touch, Kelly

158

lifted Deil's hand to her lips and seductively murmured, "Roberto, is that you?"

"Sí," an unfamiliar voice muttered.

Had her instincts been mistaken? Kelly spun around in dismay. A grinning Deil stood behind her. "Very funny!" she said. "You're lucky I didn't hit you with a box of Birds Eye, or sic the Green Giant on you!"

Deil leaned forward to bestow a quick kiss. "Your lips are cold," he complained.

"So's the rest of me. Do you want to drive or shall I?" Kelly asked, indicating the shopping basket.

"You drive."

It wasn't the first time they'd gone grocery shopping together. Deil always managed to turn the previously tiresome chore into a novel excursion. One reason for this was that Kelly never knew what unusual items he'd find to throw into the cart.

"What are we going to do with garbanzo beans?" she asked as he prepared to add a can to their cart.

"Eat them."

"We can't." She took the can out of his hands and returned it to the shelf. "Not until you eat the three cans sitting on the shelves back home!"

Deil made a big production out of rolling his eyes in exasperation.

Kelly tried to return his mind to the problem at hand. "What are we going to have for dinner?"

"Your brother's not a vegetarian, is he?"

"Tom is extremely carnivorous."

"Then how about steak?" They were now in front of the meat department.

"Ivan's the vegetarian."

"A vegetarian who's into leather?"

Kelly's only reply was a grin and a shrug.

Deil tossed the steak back. "In that case we'd better not have this." He started to turn away, but then changed his mind. "On second thought, we'll buy it now and eat it later." The plastic-wrapped package was tossed into the cart. "How about fish?" he suggested.

"Not trout," she warned.

"I know, you don't like the way they stare at you. Then how about shrimp salad?"

"Too expensive."

"I give up!"

"We'll have spaghetti," Kelly decided. "We could have two kinds of sauce, one with meat and one without." She made a quick U-turn, expertly weaved around two mulling shoppers, and then hung a sharp left.

"This isn't the Grand Prix, you know," Deil mockingly reminded her.

Two bottles of sauce were carefully placed on the kiddy seat, along with a box of thin spaghetti. A few more necessities were picked up on their way to the cashier, including a bottle of wine.

"Nebraska, 1983," Deil pretended to read the label. "Good year!"

Dinner turned out to be a huge success. Deil and Ivan exchanged a nonstop series of quips that made everyone laugh until their sides hurt. At one point the conversation swung toward semantics, with Tom challenging Deil on the definition of a certain word. Kelly had to get a dictionary to settle the matter. Deil, of course, was right. But once Tom had the reference book in hand, he didn't give up. He found numerous obscure words and requested definitions. Deil knew them all, to everyone's amazement. Even zymurgy!

160

"The branch of chemistry dealing with fermentation, as in winemaking," he defined, looking directly at Kelly when he added, "Particularly popular in Nebraska!"

"I concede defeat!" Tom laughed.

It took another thirty-six hours before Deil was able to exclaim, "Alone at last!"

Kelly turned from the window where she'd been watching her brother and his promised driver pull away in a rundown van. "Didn't you like Tom?"

"You know I did." A pair of male arms stole around her waist. "Your brother's got quite a sense of humor. Must run in the family." He dropped a kiss just beneath her earlobe. "Tom told me a lot about you."

Knowing how her brother loved to overstate the truth, Kelly was immediately concerned. "He did?"

"Mmm." Deil nuzzled her neck. "Explained a lot."

"About what?"

"Why you're not ticklish, for one thing."

"I could've told you that. With four brothers, it was simply a matter of self-preservation."

"That's not all he told me . . ." Deil tantalizingly continued both his narrative and his caresses. "I think it would be safe to say that I now know as much about you as Sally told you about me."

"I'm not sure how much of what you were told is true. Tom loves to tease."

"So do you," he muttered, catching her trailing fingers and raising them to his mouth for a chastising nibble. "Hey, where are you going?" he demanded as she slipped out of his grasp.

"I'll be right back." She returned with an armful of clean bedlinens.

"What are you doing?"

"Making the bed." She removed the couch pillows. "Care to help me?"

Deil advanced toward her with a purposeful glint in his hazel eyes. "If there's any making to be done, I think it should be me making love to you."

Kelly wholeheartedly agreed, her hugs and kisses showing her enthusiastic approval. The bed was unfolded in record time. Sheets and pillowcases tumbled to the floor, soon to be joined by a pile of clothing as an unencumbered Deil tumbled an equally freed Kelly onto the bare mattress.

CHAPTER TEN

Kelly juggled the paper bag holding dinner while aiming her key toward the lock. She didn't bother ringing the bell because she knew Deil was out, which suited her plans perfectly. Once inside the apartment, Kelly placed the white cardboard containers from the Chinese take-out place in the oven and returned to the living room.

The first item on the agenda was moving the recently bartered coffee table over to sit in front of the bay-windowed alcove. Two small pillows were then stolen from the couch and placed on the floor on either end of the table. Plates and placemats were laid out on the table along with two pairs of wooden chopsticks.

Still dripping from a quick shower, Kelly rummaged through her closet until she found was she was looking for. The peacock green shantung robe had been a Christmas present from her father's brother, a naval career man stationed in the Philippines. The robe's dramatic style wasn't suitable for everyday wear, even in Aspen! But for this evening's performance it was perfect. The thin lapels were held together by a wide sash that tied around the middle. The unknown seamstress had not been overly generous with the material. Although the label said Medium, it was smoothly stretched across Kelly's curves without an inch to spare. Her lips curved into an impish grin as she beheld her voluptuous appearance in the mirror.

Hearing the front door open and close, Kelly padded out of the bedroom in her bare feet. Deil's puzzled glance was aimed at the place settings on the coffee table, but when he turned and saw Kelly, his mouth dropped open in amazement.

"What do you call that thing you're almost wearing?"

Kelly stamped her bare foot in impatient frustration. So much for heated declarations of love! Maintaining her composure with difficulty, she politely asked, "Are you hungry?"

"Absolutely!" His initial remark may have seemed disappointingly light, but there was nothing light about his deep voice, nor the hungry way in which he looked at her. Kelly could almost feel the physical impact of his gaze, feel his eyes skimming her face, resting on her mouth, lowering to the revealing V neck of the silk robe. He certainly had the appearance of a man with a ravenous appetite, ravenous for the taste of her!

Once he was certain she'd received his intimate visual message, he spoke again, his mundane words at variance with the suggestive delivery. "What's for dinner?"

"Chinese." Her hand smoothed the silk material in an unconsciously sensuous movement. "Can't you tell?"

"I see. That's why you're wearing that exotic concoction. Quite a step up from your kamikaze kimono."

"Don't you like it?" Her innocent question was accompanied by a provocative look.

"Oh, I like it all right." His eyes darkened with unmasked passion. "Shall I show you how much?"

"After dinner," she promised, sexily sauntering toward the kitchen. "Sit down. It will be on the table in a minute."

"So will I, if I'm not careful," Deil muttered under his breath, trying to fit his long legs into a lotus position in order to sit at the low table.

Kelly transferred the food into serving dishes which sh placed on a platter along with a pot of Chinese tea. Sh carried the tray like a veteran waitress, unloading every·thing onto the table before gracefully sitting down.

"I hope you like it."

Deil helped himself to the nearest dish. "What is this?"

"Sepia kow."

"Which is?"

"Squid."

He quickly dropped the spoon back in the dish. "I think I'll pass on that one."

"I was only kidding. It's really chicken and the dark things are mushrooms. Cross my heart," she added, since he still looked suspicious.

When his plate was full, Deil picked up the wooden chopsticks. "I hope I can remember how to use these."

"I have faith in your abilities," Kelly replied, deftly picking up her own set of chopsticks. "Here, try this." She enticingly held out a piece of breaded pork.

"Mmm, it's good. Here. Your turn."

And so the meal continued, with them laughingly feed-ing each other. Since it was difficult maneuvering the food with the chopsticks, Kelly would lean forward in order to prevent any accidents. The action loosened the sash on her robe bit by bit, until the shadow between her breasts was clearly visible and Deil was made very much aware that she was wearing little, if anything, under it. While his appetite for food was satiated, his appetite for her was rapidly growing.

The next time he offered her a tidbit, he deliberately let

his hand drift to the left, swiping her cheek with sweet and sour sauce. "Let me fix that." Returning the chopsticks to his plate, he reached across the table to cup the nape of her neck and draw her closer. Once she was within kissing distance, he sensuously licked the sauce from her cheek.

"Mmm, you taste delicious," he murmured against her skin.

Kelly's only reply was an inaudible groan of hunger . . . for Deil's touch. She was unable to voice one of her customary pert rejoinders because her senses were under attack, aflame with desire.

His tongue spearheaded the sensual invasion, slowly sweeping across her cheek, flicking the tip of her nose, rolling over her parted lips. It was a slow, insidious seduction that wrapped its way around her heart with ravishing stealth. Her tongue returned his play until their mouths merged and the kiss became complete.

"Dessert?" she half-heartedly remembered as he drew her over to the couch with tantalizing kisses and embracing arms.

"Will be consumed in bed!"

The August days passed quickly. The hours slipped through her fingers, turning into days that would be forever engraved in her memory, and nights that were burned into her very soul. She loved Deil more with each day, and pushed all thought of the future out of her mind.

They were enjoying a lazy Sunday, discussing different ways of spending their evening, when Kelly came across a notice in the paper. "How about a rendezvous in the park?" Her question was accompanied by a saucy wink.

Seated beside her on the couch, Deil's eyes were full of humorous passion. "Isn't the park a little . . . public?"

She tapped the notice in the paper. "Not for a free concert, no."

"Oh, is that what you were inviting me to?"

Kelly slid her feet beneath his seated figure. "Why, what did you have in mind?"

"Entertainment of another kind!" he growled, manacling her ankles and tugging her onto his lap.

The park was within walking distance of the apartment. They set out early, strolling hand in hand, window-shopping at some of Aspen's diversified stores. One display, in an antique shop, held Kelly's attention. "I'm glad they're closed," she sighed, leaning forward to get a better look at the row of pendants resting on a velvet background.

"You're glad?" Deil repeated, uncertain that he'd heard her correctly. When she nodded, he asked, "Why's that?"

"So I won't be tempted to go inside."

"This store isn't that far from Artisans, is it?"

Kelly failed to see the connection, but she answered his question. "Just a few blocks."

"And aren't you ever tempted to stop by here on the way to the gallery?"

"I'm always late when I'm on my way to the gallery. I hate to get out of bed," she ended, her look leaving him in no doubt that he was the cause of her indolence.

"I had noticed." His look was full of loving appreciation. "What about stopping here after work then?"

"I'm too eager to get home." She ran her hand up and down his arm. "You tempt me even more than this antique shop does."

"What is it in particular that tempts you? About this shop, I meant," he clarified in response to her provocatively expressive gaze. "That umbrella stand in the corner? The brass fireplace tongs?"

Each question was greeted with a shake of her head, the silky strands of her hair flicking his cheek.

"I know, the round container with the long handle."

"Not the bedwarmer, no. I've already got one of those!"

"Oh?"

"You!" Resting her chin on the tip of his shoulder, she kissed him with winsome forwardness.

"Let's go." He tugged on her hand. "We're going to be late."

"Okay. Let me just get one more look at it."

"At what?"

"The locket."

"Locket? Which locket?"

"The one in the front row, second from the left." It was heart-shaped, with a symbolic tree of life intricately carved on its surface. The burnished gold shone with a rich patina.

"Very nice."

"And very expensive! Let's go. I want to make one more stop before the concert begins."

"Where to this time?"

Kelly guided him into a small arcade and down a short flight of steps into a gourmet ice cream shop.

"This stuff never saw Norway, you know," Deil scoffed.

"I don't care where it comes from; it tastes delicious. Uh-oh."

"Now what?" The question was asked with wry resignation, as if he were accustomed to expecting calamities when out with her.

"I left my wallet at home again."

There was something about the way Deil said "Oh" that made her ask, "What's wrong?"

"I left my wallet at home too."

"Great."

"I've got some change." He dug into his jeans pocket. Kelly did the same. "So do I."

The grand total of their net worth came to $2.87, just enough for one double ice cream soda, but not enough for two singles. "We'll share," he decided.

She checked the billboard-type menu. "We get two scoops. What flavor do you want?"

"Black cherry."

"I should've guessed," she teased, knowing that to be his favorite.

"How about you?"

"Chocolate chocolate chip."

"With black cherry?" he grimaced.

"Sure! Where's your spirit of adventure?"

"Not in my stomach."

"Can I help you?" the teenage assistant asked.

"We're not ready yet," Kelly replied.

"Yes, we are," Deil contradicted. "We'll have a double cherry ice cream soda with one scoop of black cherry and one of chocolate chocolate chip."

"In the same soda?" the assistant dubiously questioned.

"It's a fantastic combination!" Deil enthused. "Served at all the best parties in Europe. You should try it sometime."

Kelly was hard-pressed to contain her laughter at Deil's acting performance.

"What gave me away?" he wanted to know as they left the store.

"The pennies. That guy was all ready to believe your story until he saw the handful of change you gave him."

"I might have been an eccentric millionaire for all he knew."

"Perhaps if you still had your English accent, he might have been more gullible."

"Horrors! I've lost my accent? Time to go back to London!"

Deil meant it teasingly, but his words were true. There were only ten days left before his departure. *Forget it,* Kelly fiercely reminded herself, slipping her arm around his waist.

They sat out under the stars, listening to the musicians from the Aspen Music School performing classics by Aaron Copland. The music was eminently suited to their surroundings. The summer slopes, bare of snow, were only dark shapes against the chromatic twilight sky, yet their presence had an immediacy that made itself felt. In the distance were the faint outlines of the peaks of Independence Pass and the Continental Divide.

Kelly took another sip of their ice cream soda, feeling sublimely content. Deil's hand reached out to guide hers, soda and all, over to his mouth where he took the straw between his lips. There was something warmly stimulating about seeing those lips touch the same spot hers had. Sharing a straw was a simple enough occurrence, Kelly had done it numerous times in the past, but never with such an awareness of the sharing.

She knew Deil was watching the play of emotions over her face, knew he was cognizant of her thoughts. Ripples of emotion undulated between them, each one a mark of reciprocation. Eyes clung, caught up in the silent communication.

Deil released the straw from his lips and guided it back to hers for one final sip before the cup was removed from her clasp and set on the ground. Leaning forward he lightly placed his lips a mere breath away from hers. That

170

breath was lost as Kelly inhaled sharply and met his kiss. Now he tasted the lingering sweetness of their shared treat, claiming it as his own.

"You make me hear music," he leaned away to murmur with a tigerish grin.

Aware that a public park wasn't the place to continue what that kiss had started, Kelly said, "Perhaps we should go home and do a little composing of our own!"

During the next week, Deil's last in Aspen, they spent as much time together as possible. On Wednesday they spent the day up in the mountains. The late afternoon sun was warm on their bare heads as they stood atop a rocky promontory. They were both wearing denim cut-offs. Kelly's were topped by the infamous Left Bank T-shirt Deil was so fond of, while he wore a short-sleeved blue sweat shirt from his college days.

Standing a safe distance from the edge, Kelly looked down at her hiking boots in disgust. "I feel like Bigfoot," she complained.

"No, you don't," he contradicted her, stealing up from behind to wrap his arms around her waist. "You feel like a gorgeous, sexy woman!"

Kelly playfully slapped his wayward hand away from its provocative climb under her T-shirt. She'd teased him before they'd left the apartment, claiming he wouldn't be able to withstand the temptation of her T-shirt. "You claimed you could go the distance without indulging in any 'creative' n.ountain climbing!"

"So I did." Deil reluctantly lowered his hand back to her waist. "Accepting dares always did get me into trouble!"

"Then you should be more careful about what you say."

"I didn't say anything about shorts though." His incor-

171

rigible hands slid into the front pocket of her cut-offs, pulling her back to rest against him. Her curves fit spoon-fashion into his hollows, her femininity complementing his masculinity. Strong fingers investigated the ridge of her pelvic bone through the faded denim material, his touch full of love, yet without sexual demand.

They stood there for a time, at peace within themselves. "We'll have to come back here again," Kelly said without thinking.

That peace was immediately disrupted. "I have to leave in a week," Deil gently reminded her.

"I know."

"Will you be all right?" It wasn't the first time they'd discussed his departure. But this time Kelly knew by the seriousness of his tone that he wanted more than a flippant retort.

"I'll manage. I'm tough. Don't you know that?"

"I know that's what you'd like others to believe."

"But you don't buy it?"

"I'd like to think I know you rather well. And I know you're not the kind of woman who gives her love casually."

"I wouldn't say there's been anything casual about our relationship." She turned to face him. "Would you?"

"No. If I were to marry anyone, it would be you, Kelly. I'm just not ready to settle down."

"I know." She stared down at her clenched hands. "I guess we'd better start back."

"In a minute. After this."

Her head lifted. "After what?"

"This." His lips lowered to caress hers, tender in their adoration. The passionate intensity of their kiss grew until

172

Deil felt he had to remove himself from temptation.

He rested his damp forehead against hers as he muttered, "We'd probably better stop this."

"Mmm, in a minute." Kelly pulled his head back down to hers.

"If we don't stop, we're going to start a forest fire!" he warned in husky tones.

"I already feel like I've gone up in smoke!" she wryly admitted, moving away from him.

"Where there's smoke, there's fire, and speaking of such, we should get back to the picnic grounds to build ours." They had planned on having an old-fashioned wiener roast after sunset.

It was well into twilight when they got back to the picnic site. The car was only a few feet away, yet shielded from sight by a large pine. Deil brought out the grocery bag full of provisions.

"I'm starving!" Kelly tried peeking over the corrugated edge of the paper bag. "What've you got?"

"All in good time, my dear Watson," Deil affectionately rebuked, effortlessly shifting his load so that she couldn't see the contents.

"What are we going to use as cooking forks?"

"We'll use sticks, of course. This is an old-fashioned roast. Why don't you go find two suitable sticks while I start the fire. Don't go far, though," he warned. "It's getting late."

Kelly came back a few minutes later to find a respectable fire burning. "Well done, English," she congratulated him, welcoming the warmth on her still-bare legs.

"'Twas nothing," Deil modestly shrugged. "I merely rubbed two sticks together . . ."

"Two sticks, huh?" she challenged, holding up a bag of ready-start charcoal.

"Yes, well, that didn't work, so I had to enlist a little help from modern technology."

"You've got an answer for everything."

"Good thing, too, with the questions you ask. Enough of this idle chatter now, let's get cooking!"

Deil pulled out a pocketknife and efficiently whittled the sticks into sharp-tipped spears. They sat on a roughly hewn log before the fire, knees bent, shoulders touching.

"I see you like your hot dogs as well done as your toast," Kelly noted as he hungrily downed his dinner.

"You've gotten me addicted to the taste of carbon."

"Are you insulting my cooking again?"

His expression, softened by the firelight, was one of tender mockery. "Would I do a thing like that?"

"Not if you're smart, no!"

"I thought we'd already confirmed my above-average intelligence."

Kelly ignored his teasing comment. "What's for dessert?"

"It starts with an M," Deil hinted.

"Me?"

"Tempting . . ." He eyed her with unconcealed relish before shaking his head. "But not for toasting. No, we're having marshmallows for dessert."

"I haven't roasted marshmallows in years!"

"Neither have I," he confessed, spearing one of the soft white cubes with his stick and thrusting it into the fire.

"Don't tell me you like your marshmallows well done too!" she exclaimed as he pulled the burning remains out of the fire.

Deil swiftly blew out the flaming dessert and let it cool

before carefully pulling off the blackened shell and popping it into his mouth, leaving the gooey insides on the stick to be cooked again.

Kelly followed suit, making a face as she chewed. "It must be an acquired taste," she wryly decided.

They sampled a dozen more. Kelly carefully monitored the progress of her marshmallows, pulling them out when they got golden brown.

Deil watched her as she leaned toward the fire, his eyes drawn by the alluring picture she made. The flickering firelight played over her face, highlighting her cheekbones, softening her profile.

The plaid blanket was drawn capelike around both of them, protecting their backs from the chilly night air. It was a simple matter for Deil to slip his arm under the blanket and pull her close. Not anticipating his move, Kelly reached out to balance herself, her palm coming into contact with his bare knee. The warmth of his body seemed like friendly territory waiting to be explored, so she did so, her fingers stroking their way up his thigh.

Her voice was a study of feminine seduction as she murmured, "I like your legs, English."

"The feeling is mutual!" Deil's hand glided up the curvature of her leg, from ankle to knee, knee to thigh.

"Nice knees," she complimented. "Ever consider modeling?"

"You have such a saucy wit!" he growled menacingly.

Even in the dim light Deil could see the mischief in her eyes as she asked, "Is that all I've got?"

"If one discounts your gorgeous body . . ."

"Sorry, no discounts," she inserted.

"And your obvious talents."

"Talents? Are we talking about the art of stained glass?"

"No, we're talking about the art of making love."

Her eyes widened with feigned ingenuousness. "We are?"

"Mmm, and that's the problem. We're talking when a demonstration would be much more effective—and enjoyable!"

The passionate power of his embrace brought them both to the ground, resting on a bed of fallen pine needles. Caught up in the spell of his kiss, bewitched by the magic of his caressing hands, it took a while for the subtle discomfort to get through. When it did so, Kelly's muttered "Ouch!" held an almost startled quality.

"Did I hurt you?" Deil leaned away to question in concern.

"Not you, no. The damn pine needles hurt me! I thought the forest floor was supposed to be a veritable carpet of softness. No one ever warned me about getting pricked with sharp needles or rolling over hard pine cones."

"Some things have to be experienced firsthand for their true importance to be felt."

"It's been felt!" she emphatically confirmed as yet another needle pricked her.

"Then I vote that we temporarily adjourn these proceedings for the twenty minutes it will take us to drive straight home. All in favor?"

"Aye!"

"The ayes carry it with one abstaining vote from the raccoon behind the tree over there."

"An abstaining raccoon? Where?"

"Never mind, we're going home."

The darkness hid Kelly's sudden sadness. If only her apartment really were Deil's permanent home, a home he'd never leave, a home where they would always be together.

CHAPTER ELEVEN

The days trickled down to mere hours and then it was time. Time for Deil to leave. He'd done all his own packing with the efficiency that was second-nature to him. Meanwhile, Kelly, as unorganized as ever, lost several of his socks as she carried the laundry basket from the front door to the bedroom. An intensive search finally located the delinquent footwear under the couch.

Their gaiety on that last day was forced, their humor a deliberate veil to cover the true intensity of their feelings. Catching his occasional glances of concern, Kelly was more determined than ever to keep up her cheerful front. She didn't want him remembering her as a tearful limpet, vainly clinging to him.

At least she would be able to accompany Deil to Denver, rather than saying good-bye in Aspen. It had been his suggestion that she accompany him, since she'd mentioned needing a new supply of glass from a Denver dealer. Kelly had even obtained special permission allowing her to return the rental Chevette in his place. This variance was only granted because she knew the owner of the rental agency. She'd done some work for him, restoring his Victorian home.

Finally they got down to the final checklist after loading the car.

"Have you got all your floppy diskettes?"

"They're in Ozzie's case."

"Your ticket?"

"In my jacket pocket."

"You'll remember to call me once you've arrived in London?" This was the one concession she'd made, allowing herself the luxury of hearing his voice again, of knowing that he'd landed safely.

"I'll call you the moment I get home."

Home. That simple Freudian slip told her that Deil still considered London to be his home.

"Shall we be off?" he asked, unaware he'd said anything amiss.

"Sure." Kelly's voice lacked its customary jauntiness.

They used the most direct route to Denver, which was over the twelve-thousand-foot Independence Pass. Although they'd driven along this road before, stopping for picnics and mountain hikes, this was the first time they'd driven all the way to the top and over. Memories floated through Kelly's mind as they passed familiar sights—the campground where they'd had their old-fashioned weiner roast, the turn-off they'd taken to go exploring. As they got higher they passed the ghost town of Independence. Its abandoned shacks seemed on the brink of collapse when compared to those of restored Ashcroft. More memories came to mind: Deil playing the cowboy, tossing his imaginary Stetson out the window and sweeping her into his arms.

Deil's voice brought her out of her reverie. "Do we have time to stop?" While she'd been immersed in thought, they'd reached the pass.

Kelly checked her watch before answering. "For a few minutes."

They got out and walked around a bit. The incisive coldness really required more protection than the trench coat Deil wore, but he seemed indifferent to the frigid temperatures. He walked ahead to read the informational placard about the Continental Divide while Kelly stayed near the car.

Bleakly hugging herself while stomping her feet, she looked at the arctic-like tundra and saw nothing but the barrenness of her own future. These mountains weren't dependent upon greenery, but without it they lacked something. So too would her life lack something without Deil's presence. She would survive, she would go on, but she'd never be the same.

Kelly shivered as the cold wind wrapped itself around her. Winter was in the air. *The winter of my discontent,* Kelly thought solemnly. "You're getting morbid," she angrily muttered under her breath. "Time to go," she shouted to Deil.

They arrived at the airport with plenty of time to spare. Deil checked in his luggage and then they wandered around the terminal, superficially looking at the souvenir shops.

"Would you like to stop for an ice cream?" Deil inquired, catching sight of a specialty eatery.

"Sure!" Kelly was filled with artificial brightness, her manner too buoyant.

She ordered one scoop of Oreo cracker ice cream. Deil predictably requested black cherry. A table near the window became vacant, so they sat there.

"Good timing. We're lucky to have gotten a place to sit down. It's awfully crowded in here." Kelly knew she was babbling, but couldn't help herself. She felt as though her life were disintegrating before her very eyes. It was there in the awkward silence that had to be filled with inane conversation. It was there in the need to pretend at all costs that everything was fine, when in fact it was not, and never would be again.

"Denver's one of my favorite airports." With that her conversational skills dried up, shriveled into meaningless phrases.

It was almost a relief when they headed for the departure area, because Kelly knew she wouldn't be able to keep up her composure for much longer. Cracks were already beginning to make themselves felt deep within her, threatening to release a lava flow of pain.

"I'll leave you here," she abruptly stated as they reached the security checkpoint. "My glass supplier is expecting me." It was a lie and it may have sounded callous, but she no longer cared. Anything was better than breaking down and clinging to him, begging him to stay.

Deil looked somewhat surprised but made no protest. Now that the moment had come, he was at a loss as to what to say. Good-bye seemed inadequate, and so final. Instead, he substituted, "Well, then . . . I'll be seeing you."

No, you won't! she felt like screaming. *You'll never see me again; you'll forget all about me the minute you step on that plane.* Aloud she simply said, "Good-bye."

She almost broke down when Deil gathered her into a tight embrace for one final kiss. His lips parted hers in a passionate exchange that was tinged with desperation. It was a kiss that told of their love, eloquently stating what they would, or could, not.

"Have a good trip," Kelly choked, tearing herself out of his arms and fleeing.

Tears burned her eyes, fogging her vision and forcing her to duck into the washroom to do something to stem the salty flow. Bathing her face with cool water, taking deep breaths, emptying her mind, it was the only way to cope with the unendurable pain.

Kelly numbly returned to the multilevel parking garage where they'd left the rented Chevette. There, on the dashboard, was an envelope with her name written on it. She recognized the bold handwriting immediately; Deil had a funny way of making his y's. Kelly remembered teasing him about it. He'd growled in response and pulled her onto the bed to make love to her.

Her hand shook as she reached out and opened the envelope with the utmost care, treating the bond paper as though it were a piece of delicate glass. Inside was a single sheet of stationery and an article wrapped in tissue paper. Kelly unfolded the letter and began reading.

Darling—It occurs to me that I never called you that. I suppose I was too busy teasing you, or making love to you, to indulge in romantic endearments. I'm sorry about that.

I thought that I might find it easier to tell you how much you mean to me if I wrote it, since this is my home turf, so to speak. Instead, I find myself unable to say how much you've enriched my life. I knew if I left you a present you'd probably refuse it, fiercely accusing me of paying for services rendered, or some such ridiculous thing. Nothing could be further from the truth. I love you, so please accept the enclosed as a token of that love. Deil.

She carefully unwrapped the tissue paper to discover a

182

locket, the very locket she'd admired in the Aspen antique shop ten days ago. The heart-shaped pendant hung from an intricate gold chain. Biting back a sob, Kelly fastened the chain at her neck. The locket nestled just beneath her collarbone, as if coming home.

Home! Kelly turned the ignition, and the Chevette jumped to life. *Home! You have to go home!* The words chased themselves around her head, erasing all thought of picking up her supplies. She reversed out of the parking stall and got on the exit ramp leading out of the garage.

The car seemed as eager to get back to the mountains as Kelly was. It went on automatic pilot, merging onto the expressway heading for the Front Range. It then bypassed the Independence Pass turn-off in favor of the longer route via Glenwood Springs, a safer choice in view of the impending darkness.

So intent was she on seeking the refuge of her apartment that Kelly forgot all about turning the car in, leaving it parked out front instead. Entering the darkened room, she rejected the light switches in favor of the anonymous blackness. Now she could let loose. There was no one to see her pain, no one to hear her tearing sobs. No one at all.

Like a wound left untreated, the ultimate pain was made more intense for having been pushed aside too long. All those weeks she'd delayed her despair, kept up the front. Now everything rushed together, silently building to form an emotional avalanche. Her hands clenched in despair at the thought of Deil aboard that plane, taking him thousands of miles from her, a little farther every minute, every second.

Deil was indeed on the wide-bodied plane, but the plane

183

itself was still on the ground. It wasn't until he'd actually boarded that he realized Kelly had let him leave so easily because she loved him. She'd given him his freedom. The ironic thing was, now that he had it, he wasn't at all sure it was what he wanted after all.

In his mind's eye he went over the scrapbook of his memories, recalling the small, abstract things that, when put together, presented a whole picture. And the picture forming was that of a life without Kelly. A dreary winter in London without her warm sense of humor, her lovely smile, her teasing understanding, her practical advice.

Caught up in his thoughts, Deil didn't realize that the plane had been sitting in its position at the gate far longer than was customary. This was also after a long delay before they'd been allowed to board.

"Ladies and gentlemen, this is your captain speaking. We're running into slight technical difficulties that are delaying our departure. Our ground crew hopes to have the matter rectified soon. Until that time, we ask that you refrain from smoking, as the no-smoking sign is still lit. Thank you for your patience and understanding."

The announcement was greeted by a rumble of dissatisfaction among the passengers. Deil paid little attention. His thoughts were still focused on Kelly, on the way they'd made love last night, on the way she'd looked at him while saying good-bye, the way she'd kissed him before turning and leaving.

His love for her wasn't in question, neither was hers for him. *Then what is the question?* he bitterly asked himself. *What are you doing here on your way out of the country, leaving the woman you love behind?* Suddenly the answer was very clear. He loved his freedom, yes, but he loved

Kelly more! The next question was how to get off this damned plane.

Fate handily provided an answer to that one in the guise of another announcement by a harried stewardess. "I'm sorry for the delay, the malfunction has turned out to be more serious than anticipated. I'm afraid we're going to have to switch to another aircraft. Please gather all your hand luggage and personal belongings before deplaning . . ."

Deil didn't even listen to the rest of the announcement. Grabbing Ozzie and his trench coat, he jostled his way through the other passengers with an uncharacteristic lack of courtesy.

"Excuse me, sir, but the departure lounge is this way," an airline representative pointed out.

"I'm not going on the flight," Deil curtly replied.

"The delay will only be a few minutes more . . ."

But Deil was already out of earshot, on his way back up the concourse. He kept up his near-running pace until he reached the ticket desk for Aspen's commuter airline. "I want to buy a seat on your next flight to Aspen."

"I'm sorry, sir," the agent regretfully said. "Our last flight departed ten minutes ago. There won't be another one until tomorrow morning."

Deil couldn't wait that long. He pivoted and strode over to the first rent-a-car desk he came to. "I want to rent a car."

"Certainly, sir," a leggy blonde smiled. "What kind of car?"

"I don't care."

"Did you want a subcompact, a compact, a—"

"A compact will be fine," he interrupted. "I don't care.

Whatever takes the least amount of time to get ready. I'm in a hurry!"

"Do you have a credit card?"

Deil whipped out his American Express card.

"If you'll just fill out your name and address on this form, I'll get the keys for you."

Deil wrote so quickly that the information was barely legible. He grabbed the keys, already on his way even as the agent was calling out the directions to the car's pick-up point.

Exhausted by her extended bout of weeping, Kelly finally fell into an exhausted slumber sometime after one A.M. She lay curled up on the unfolded Hide-a-bed, her fist pressed to her mouth, as though even in sleep she was fighting back tears. The click of the deadbolt lock being opened did not awaken her, nor did the muffled sound of approaching footsteps. It was the sound of a voice that made her heavy eyelids flicker. The sound of Deil's voice saying "Darling."

Don't wake up, she groggily warned herself. *This is a dream, and if you wake up it will be over.* She quickly closed her eyes, and was rewarded by the sound of his voice again. Drifting back to sleep, she could almost feel the touch of his hand stroking her cheek, the brush of his lips drifting across her forehead. Almost? God, it felt real! Her hand reached out to pull her dream closer. A second later she was being half-crushed by a very real male body.

"Haven't we done this before?" a masculine voice murmured against her ear.

"Deil?" It came out as a strangled gasp.

"Who else were you expecting?" he asked just as he had the first time he'd come to her bedroom.

"Are you real?" Her hands ran up and down the length of his arm for tangible reassurance.

"Don't I feel real?" He lowered himself more intimately against her.

"What are you doing here?" Her tone was one of utter confusion. "Aren't you supposed to be halfway over the Atlantic by now?"

"I forgot something."

Her heart dropped like a stone. So that's why he'd come back. It must have been something extremely important for him to have gotten off the plane and come all the way back to Aspen. "What did you forget?"

"You."

The lingering traces of drowsiness left her eyes as they popped open. "Me?"

He nodded, tenderly caressing her face. "When it came down to the crunch, I couldn't leave. My freedom seemed meaningless, my independence a mockery. I'm only free when you're with me, only independent when you're by my side."

"Oh, Deil!" Her voice cracked at his simple eloquence.

"Can you forgive me for being so stupid? For coming so close to letting you go, to losing you?"

"There's nothing to forgive." She threw her arms around his neck. "It was a decision only you could make, whether to leave or whether to stay. It killed me to stand back and not interfere, but I had to give you space."

"I don't need space. In fact, at the moment there's too much of it between you and me."

His nimble fingers unbuttoned her cotton blouse, tugging it from the waistband of her denim skirt.

Kelly returned the favor, freeing the buttons of his Oxford-cloth shirt while confessing, "I thought I'd never see you again."

"You'll see me. Didn't you notice that I never said good-bye? I said 'I'll be seeing you.' And I will. Seeing . . ." His hazel eyes were unguarded, intimate and warm. ". . . and feeling all of you."

Once freed from the constricting confines of their clothes, they were able to caress each other at will. Eyes beckoned, hands tempted, lips tasted. Their kiss was exquisitely long in duration and rapturously fierce in intensity, reflecting as it did the depth of their requited love.

Breaking off to draw in oxygen, she felt Deil trembling as he buried his face in her hair. "God, I love you."

"And I love you," she murmured. "So very much." Kelly enticingly reacquainted herself with the beloved terrain of his body, her hands climbing over the muscular planes of his back before gliding down the long indentation of his spine. She loved every inch of him, gloried in the power of his masculinity.

With a heartfelt groan, Deil hooked one bare leg across both of hers, anchoring her to the bed. His fingers skied down the slope of her hip, tantalizingly placing their tactile caresses at deliberately erotic intervals. Explosive charges of hungry desire were shooting all along her nervous system.

Purrs of pleasure were interspersed with pledges of love as each of them searched and found the answering chord in the other. Closing the gap between them, Deil intimately came to her and was welcomed with open arms. Her fingers drove into the rippling muscles of his back as Kelly met his delicious possession, matching it with seductive demands of her own.

This time was unlike any other, marked by passionate

volitility rather than sensuous deliberation. Their ascension was incandescently rapid, bringing them to the very apex of desire. Intimately joined together, they hovered at the edge of the universe, poised on the brink of boundless satisfaction. A moment later Deil's surging motions sent her soaring once more; soaring into an uninterrupted flight that was rhythmically breathtaking and mindlessly impassioned.

It was some time before either one of them was in anything even approaching a coherent state. When they were able to speak clearly, Kelly was astonished to hear Deil ask, "When's the wedding?"

"Wedding?" she drowsily repeated. "What wedding?"

"Our wedding."

"I thought you couldn't afford the responsibilities of marriage."

"I can't afford to lose you."

"What ever happened to 'have word processor, will travel'?"

"I may never move again," Deil murmured in what sounded suspiciously like the purr of a jungle cat.

"You may have to," she softly laughed as the phone began to ring. "You'll have to answer it."

"Let it ring."

"It may be important. Three A.M. is a strange time for someone to be calling."

He finally picked up the receiver on the twentieth ring, barking "Hello" into the mouthpiece.

"Deil?"

"Sally?"

"Guess what? Andrew and I are getting married!"

"So are we!" he returned.

"You and Kelly?" Even over the crackly static on the

189

line, Sally's surprised delight was clearly audible as she said, "Congratulations!"

"The same to you."

"Hey, wait a minute!" In her hurried excitement to share her good news with Kelly, Sally had lost touch with reality for a moment. "I'm supposed to be picking you up at the airport in an hour."

"Forget it," he laconically advised. "I'll let you know what our plans are. We'll call you later. Bye, Sally."

Deil turned back to Kelly. "Now, where were we?"

"I believe you were saying that you may never move again."

"Mmm, that's right." He settled beside her, pressing her against him. "I may never move again."

"No?" she challenged, provocatively teasing him with her fingers as well as her words.

"You talked me into it," he muttered, twisting to pin her body to his. "Care to accompany me on a little flight to the stars?"

"With you, anytime!"

Together they embarked on a sensual flight plan that would never run out of steam, for it was fueled by love!